Obliterated
PEOPLE

Pawankumar Rai

BlueRoseONE.com
Stories Matter

First Published in Februrary 2023

ISBN: 978-93-5704-887-3

BLUEROSE PUBLISHERS

www.BlueRoseONE.com

info@bluerosepublishers.com

+91 8882 898 898

Cover Design:

Pawankumar Rai and Yash

Reviewed and Edited By:

Srishti Mehrotra and Bisma Waheed

Typographic Design:

Tanya Raj Upadhyay

Distributed by: BlueRose, Amazon, Flipkart

"Warriors seek a challenging foe, as fighting the pathetic does not bring about any justice. No matter how difficult the fight, the warriors learn to persevere until they defeat all the obstacles in their path."

Pawankumar Rai

(Researcher by profession, writer by heart)

“This book is dedicated to my warrior heart parents.”

*

I must admit that after traveling a great distance to deliver Vishvesh Sudarshana's manuscript to his father, I was still a little dubious about its genuineness. Since, I could not help but think back to the short time Vishvesh had spent as one of his alumni and a most infamous practical joker. The fact is that while I sat in the Sudarshana library in Banaras, I started to feel a little silly and wished that I had just sent the manuscript by express rather than bringing it myself. I must admit that I don't like getting teased. When the joke is not on me, I have a sharp sense of humor.

Nearly every hour, Mr. Sudarshana, Sr., was anticipated. The latest steamer from New Delhi had brought news of the departure schedule of his yacht Jalayana, which was now twenty-four hours late. Since he knew his employer well enough to be certain that nothing short of a supernatural event would prevent him from carrying out what he had planned to do, Mr. Sudarshana's assistant secretary, who had been left at home, assured me that Jalayana had sailed as promised. I was also aware that the Jalayana's transmission was sealed and would only be activated in an emergency. Therefore, the only thing left to do was wait, so we did.

We spoke about the document and made educated guesses about it and the bizarre occurrences it described. It was well known that the ship INS Sudarshana, Jr., that had taken sail to India to join the Indian Ambulance had been torpedoed. I had further confirmed by wire to the owner's New Delhi headquarters that Miss Pinal headquarters that had been chartered for passage. Additionally, neither she nor Vishvesh's names appeared on the list of survivors, and neither of their bodies were found.

Their adventures during the dangerous cruise, that Modi's treachery and deceit extended until they found themselves in the waters of the far South of Indian Ocean with depleted supplies and poisoned water-casks. Their rescue by the Indian tug was a foregone conclusion; the capture of the enemy PLA-33 by the tug's crew was not out of the question.

Despite being attested by a renowned navigator from the eighteenth century, Swaraj Dweep has long been more or less legendary place. However, Vishvesh's account made it seem quite real, despite the fact that there were several miles of trackless ocean between us and it. Yes, the story left us in suspense. We both agreed that it was extremely unlikely, but neither of us could rule out any of the information it contained. The unusual plants and animals of Aadra were as possible in the thick, warm atmosphere of the super-heated crater as they were in the Tretha yuga under nearly identical conditions, which were presumably present throughout the Earth at the time.

The assistant secretary acknowledged that he had heard of Pingala and his discoveries but had never placed much weight in either. We all agreed that the one that stated a complete absence of human children in one of the tribes Sudarshana had contact with was the one that was the most difficult to explain. The manuscript's lone incoherent statement was this one. Adults rule the world! It was not doable.

We made assumptions about Agnivesh and the likely fate of his crew of Mauritian sailors'. Two of their graves were discovered by Sudarshana; how many more could have died? And Miss Pinal, after being cut off from everyone of her own kind, could a young girl have long survived the horrors of Aadra? The assistant secretary questioned whether Dhani was still with her, and we both grinned at this implied admission of the veracity of the entire strange story:

The assistant secretary commented, “I realize I'm a fool”, “but by Ghosh, I can't help believing that, and I can see that girl now, with the giant Airedale by her side guarding her from the dangers of million years ago. I can picture the entire scene, including the apelike Aadivasi men huddled in their filthy caves, the enormous pterodactyls soaring through the dense air on their bat-like wings, the powerful dinosaurs moving their cumbersome hulks beneath the shadows of preglacial forests, and the dragons that we once thought were myths until science revealed that they were the real memories of the first man, passed down through the ages by word of mouth".

If true, it is astounding, I retorted. "And to think that perhaps Sudarshana and Miss Pinal are still there, amidst horrifying threats, and that Agnivesh and some of his groups are still alive! I keep hope that Vishvesh and the girl have located the remaining survivors since. According to what Vishvesh knew at the time, there were only six of them left in total: the engineer Kumar, Agnivesh, Sharma, Saxena, Sundar, and Bhaskar. If they could band together, there might have been some hope for them;

however, if they were apart, I fear they wouldn't last very long."

"If only they hadn't let the Pakistani detainees to take control of the PLA-33! Vishvesh should have used better judgment before placing any kind of trust in them. The possibility is that the patron returned to Swaraj safely and is currently flaunting an Swastik Cross. There is no reason why they couldn't have crossed the underwater tunnel behind the barrier cliffs and made escape with a substantial supply of oil from the wells they located in Aadra sufficient water, and enough supplies."

The assistant secretary responded, "I don't like 'em," but occasionally you need to hand it to 'em.

I snarled, "Yes, and presenting to them would make me happier than anything else!" After that, the phone rang.

The assistant secretary responded, and as I observed him, I noticed that his face turned white and his mouth dropped. He hung up the receiver as if in a trance, saying, "My God!" "It's impossible!"

“What”, I questioned.

He replied in a monotone, "Mr. Sudarshana is dead.” “He passed away suddenly yesterday at sea.”

The following ten days were spent planning Mr. Vishvesh J. Sudarshana, Sr.'s funeral. The late Mr. Sudarshana's secretary, Mr. Krishna Bisht, handled everything. He is the personification of power, drive, initiative, and wisdom. I've never seen a young man with such energy. The same way a sculptor uses his modeling clay, he managed attorneys, judges, and executors. He molded, shaped, and coerced them to conform to his wishes. Before that, he had been a destitute and careless cow-puncher on one of the illustrious Sudarshana farms. He had been Vishvesh Sudarshana's college classmate and a fraternity member.

Bisht was chosen by Sudarshana Sr. out of thousands of workers, or more accurately, Sudarshana gave him the chance, and Bisht took it and made himself. Because Sudarshana, Jr. was as good as his father. However, Bisht lacked any sycophancy or fawning.

Normally, I don't wax lyrical about men, but this man comes the closest to my idea of what a typical man should be of any I have ever encountered. I risk a prediction that before Vishvesh J. Sudarshana sent him to college, he had never even heard the word ethics. At the same time, I'm equally confident that throughout his life, he has never broken a single rule of the Indian gentleman's code of ethics.

We raced out into the Pacific in quest of Swaraj Dweep ten days after they removed Mr. Sudarshana's body from the Jalayana. The Jalayana's master and crew were among the forty people in the group, and Bisht the Indomitable was in charge. We had a drawn-out and boring hunt for Swaraj Dweep since the outdated map the assistant secretary had used to find it was wildly wrong. We were so far south that it was unclear whether we were in the Indian ocean or the Pacific when its forbidding walls eventually emerged from the ocean's mists in front of us. It was really chilly and there were many bergs.

Throughout the journey, Bisht had persistently avoided questions about how we were to enter Aadra once we had discovered Swaraj Dweep. The sole entrance or exit to the crater world were beyond the impregnable cliffs is the underground outflow of the Aadraian River, which was made abundantly clear to everyone by Vishvesh Sudarshana's text. The Jalayana could have soared over the cliffs just as easily as it could have sailed beneath them. Sudarshana's group had been able to cross this channel because their vessel had been a submarine.

Farhan and Naagar wasted many hours coming up with creative solutions to get past the barrier cliffs and placing crazy bets on which one Krishna Bisht was considering. However, as soon as we were all confident that we had reached Swaraj Dweep, Bisht gathered us all together.

Until we discovered the island, he claimed, there was no point in discussing these issues. Until we are able to closely examine the shore, it can only be at best our conjecture. From Vishvesh's text, each of us has created a mental image of the Pingalaan seacoast, and it is unlikely that any two of these images would match one another or the coast as we will soon discover it. I have three ideas on how to climb the cliffs, and each one has the necessary gear in the grasp.

When the Jalayana is anchored at a safe distance from land, there is an electric drill with enough waterproof cable to reach from the ship's dynamos to the cliff's top, and there is enough half-inch iron rod to construct a ladder from the base to the cliff's top. Boring the holes and inserting the ladder rungs from the bottom up would be a difficult, risky task, but it is possible.

I also have a life-saving mortar that we could use to cast a line over the cliff's summit, but this plan would require one of us to climb to the top, increasing the likelihood that the line would break at the summit or the hooks at the upper end would slip. I think my third strategy is the most doable.

Before we sailed, you all witnessed several sizable, weighed boxes being lowered into the hold. I can tell you did because you inquired about what they contained and made a comment about the big 'H' emblazoned on each box. These boxes contain different components of a hydro-aeroplane.

If there is enough room above high waters, I intend to erect this on the section of beach mentioned in Vishvesh's manuscript–the sand where he discovered the apelike man's dead body. If not, we will have to assemble it on deck and lower it over the side. Once it is put together, I will haul ropes and tackle to the top of the cliff, where it will be quite easy to hoist the search party and its supplies in safety. Alternatively, I can make enough visits to drop the entire party off in the valley beyond the barrier; everything will, of course, rely on the results of my initial reconnaissance.

We moved slowly that afternoon along the imposing barrier of Swaraj Dweep.

As we craned our necks to look up at the summit thousands of feet above us, Bisht said, "You see now how foolish it would have been to squander our time hammering out details of a plan to surpass those." He then jerked his thumb in the direction of the cliffs. "To build a ladder to the summit would take weeks or even months. I was completely unaware of impressive height. A line extended halfway to the peak of the lowest point would not be supported by our mortar. Discussing any other plan besides the hydro-aeroplane is pointless. We'll locate the beach and start moving."

Late the next morning, the lookout said there was surf about a mile ahead, and as we got closer, we all noticed that the line to breaks had been broken by a long sweep of rolling surf on a small beach. Five of us landed on the landing strip once it was dropped, getting soaked in the icy seas in the process. However, we were rewarded with the cleanly selected bones of what may have been the skeleton of a very low order of man or a high order of ape near to the cliff's base.

After making a choice, Bisht acted quickly. As a result, by mid-afternoon, we had all of the large boxes marked "H" on the beach and were actively working on to open them.

The plane was put together and tuned for two complete days. We filled it with ropes and tackles, water, food, and ammunition, and then we individually begged Bisht to let us go with him. But he refused to listen any. That was Bisht; he always performed any really volunteered for challenging or hazardous activities that required just one man to do. He never asked for volunteers when he needed help; instead, he chose the man or men he thought were most suited for the job. According to him, all volunteer service is based on fundamentally flawed notions, and he believed that the command's decision to call for volunteers was a testament to its leadership and loyalty.

Bisht mounted the pilot's seat once we moved the aircraft down to the water's edge. He took a moment to make sure he had everything before continuing. Farhan double-checked his arsenal and supply of ammunition to be sure nothing was missing. Along with the handgun and rifle, the machine gun positioned in front of him on the aircraft also had ammunition for the other two weapons.

We were all deeply moved by Vishvesh's description of the horrors of Aadra and the need for suitable defense measures. All was finally prepared. We pushed the plane out into the surf after starting the motor. She was skimming toward the sea a short while later. She slowly emerged from the water's surface, quickly mounted, performed a wide spiral, circled high above us, and then vanished beyond the cliffs' crest. We were all waiting in silence, eyes fixed on the imposing summit above us. Hollis, who was now in charge, frequently checked his wristwatch.

Goodness, Short cried, "we ought to hear from him pretty soon!"

Farhan chuckled apprehensively. He had just been gone for ten minutes, he declared. It feels like an hour, Naagar remarked. "What is that? You heard that, right? He's shooting! Machine gun, that is! Oh, Lord, and here we are, ten thousand miles away, as helpless as a bunch of old ladies! Nothing can be done by us. We have no idea what is going on. Why wouldn't he allow one of us to accompany him?"

Yes, the machine gun did it. It would be audible to us clearly for at least one minute. Then silence followed. This occurred two weeks ago. Since then, Krishna Bisht hasn't given us any indications or signals.

****

*

I will always remember how Aadra initially struck me as I circled in high over the surrounding rocks. I peered down at the hazy ground below me from the plane through the mist. A thin ribbon of vapour is sent far out across the Indian subcontinent when the hot, humid atmosphere of Aadra condenses while being fanned by the frigid Indian ocean air-currents that sweep across the crater's surface. Through this, the image suggested a massive impressionistic canvas filled with blobs of colour emerging through the falling mist, encircling the deep blue of the inland sea with greens, browns, scarlets, and yellows.

I dropped close to the cliffs and skirted them for several kilometres before swinging back down in search of a clearing close to the base of the massive escarpment, but I was unable to locate one with a large enough clearing to ensure safety. By this point, I was flying very low and scanning the ground below me for potential landing sites as well as wildlife. I could tell the water surface was absolutely black with critters of some kind until I reached pretty deep towards the southern end of the island, where an arm of the lake goes far inland. I was too high up to distinguish between specific people, but the overall image was of a huge army of amphibious creatures. The land was almost equally alive with things that crawled, leaped, ran, and flew. While I was focused on the strange scene below, it was one of the latter that almost killed me.

I first became aware of it when the sunlight suddenly vanished from above, and as I swiftly glanced up, I saw a fantastic monster swooping down on me. With an equal spread of wings, it must have measured a full eighty feet from the tip of its thick, short tail to the end of its long, horrible beak. It was hissing horribly and charging directly towards me; I could hear it above the propeller's spin. I let it have it square in the breast as it came straight down into the machine gun's muzzle, but it continued to pursue me, forcing me to dive and turn even though I was perilously close to the ground.

The object didn't miss me by more than a dozen feet, and when I rose, it wheeled and followed me-but only until it reached the cooler air near the clifftops, where it then turned and fell. I was driven to go after it by something, maybe the human desire for conflict and the thrill of the chase, so I circled and dove as well. The thing came after me once more as soon as I descended into Aadra's comfortable atmosphere, rising above me to swoop down on me. Nothing could have been more appropriate for my arsenal given that my machine gun was aimed skyward at a 45° angle and could not be raised or lowered by the pilot. The large reptile could have been raked from nearly any position if I had a companion with me, but because the thing always attacked from above, he always found me ready with a hail of shots. Before the monster abruptly turned completely over in the air and crashed to the ground, the combat had to have lasted for at least a minute.

We shared a room at college, and Vishvesh taught me a lot of things that weren't covered in my usual classes. Despite his love of entertainment, he was a reasonably excellent student, and his main interest was granthgyan. I was familiar with the fish, amphibians, reptiles, and mammals of the Tretha age since he used to tell me about the many animal and plant life forms that had once blanketed the earth. I recognized what had attacked me; Sarppakshi: meaning flying snakes, which should have gone extinct millions of years ago. I only had to look at it to understand that Vishvesh had not exaggerated anything in his book.

After eliminating my first enemy, I started looking for a landing spot close to the base of the cliffs where my party was waiting for me. The Sarppakshi's carcass had hardly fallen when I was surrounded by at least a dozen of those repulsive creatures, some large and some small but all intent on my destruction. I knew how anxious my companions would be for a word from me and I was equally anxious to ease their minds and to get them and our supplies well within Aadra, so that we could set off on our mission of finding and rescuing Vishvesh Sudarshana.

I quickly moved from among them to the cooler strata where they dared not follow because I was unable to handle them all. Then I remembered that Vishvesh's account explicitly stated that the further north one travelled in Aadra, the fewer the terrifying reptiles were that made human life on the southern end of the island impossible. There seemed to be no other option at this point but to look for a more northerly landing spot, find the Jalayana, and take my comrades two at a time over the cliffs and to the rendezvous. I was tempted to go exploring as I flew north. With less gas than I had in my tanks, I figured I could easily cover Aadra and get back to the shore. There was also a chance I would run across Vishvesh or any of his party.

I was drawn out into the wide length of inland sea, and as I did so, I noticed islands at either end of the large body of water, one to the south and one to the north. However, I did not change my path to get closer to either island; I saved that for a later time.

Although it was a hillier and more open country, the farther coast of the sea exposed a considerably narrower strip of land between the cliffs and the water than upon the western side. There were beautiful landing areas, and I thought I saw a village off in the distance to the north, but I wasn't sure. But as I got closer to the area, I noticed several human figures pursuing what appeared to be one person who had run across a huge meadow. They heard the spinning of my propellers and looked above as I descended to have a closer look at these people. They briefly stood still, pursuers and chased, before breaking away and running towards the nearest wood cover. There were flying reptiles even in this area of Aadra, I realised this as a large bulk almost immediately swooped down upon me. The beast dove for my right wing so swiftly that the only thing that could have saved me was a precipitous drop. My technique was highly risky because I was already close to the earth, but I was on the verge of pulling it off when I realised that I was getting too close to a big tree. I failed miserably in my attempt to avoid both the tree and the pterodactyl at the same time. When one wing contacted an upper limb, the plane dipped, spun around, and then, out of control, slammed into the tree branches, coming to rest 40 feet above the ground, bruised and ripped.

The enormous reptile circled twice above me while hissing loudly before taking off in the direction of the south. My plane got stuck in the tree when it came close to it. Forests are the safest haven from these, as I suspected at the time and would later learn. Unattractive creatures that, because to their wide wing spread and substantial weight, look just as out of place among trees as a seaplane does.

I clutched to my battered flyer for about a minute, my mind paralysed by the terrifying calamity that had befallen me and rendering it unusable beyond repair. This craft had been the foundation of every strategy I had for helping Vishvesh and Miss Pinal, and in a matter of minutes, my own narcissistic love of adventure had dashed both of our expectations. I couldn't even begin to imagine what impact that might have on how the rescue mission will ultimately turn out. Their lives might be sacrificed as a result of my suicidal stupidity. Although it appeared obvious that I was doomed, I can honestly state that my friends' futures were more important to me than my own.

As I was leaving, my party was anxiously anticipating my arrival across the barrier rocks. They would soon be overcome with anxiety and panic, and they wouldn't even realise it! I was certain that they would try to climb the cliffs, but I wasn't so sure they would succeed. After some time, the survivors would turn around and make their way back home in a dejected and sorrowful manner. Home! Since I should never again see home, I tried to set my jaws and block out the term.

What about Vishvesh and his girlfriend? They too were doomed by me. They wouldn't even be aware that a rescue attempt had been made. If they were still alive, they might come across the wreckage of this large plane hanging in its lofty tomb one day and speculate inanely and be amazed, but they would never know, and I could not help but be relieved that they would not be aware that Krishna Bisht had sealed their death warrants through his heinous selfishness.

All of these pointless regrets were making me feel awful, but eventually I shook myself free of them, made an effort to forget them, accepted the circumstances as they were, and did everything I could to turn defeat into success. I was severely shaken up and wounded, but I thought I was extremely fortunate to survive. I had to ascend from the plane into the tree and then down to the ground carefully and at great risk due to the perilous angle at which it hung. My situation was dire. Between me and my buddies was an inland sea that was at this time sixty miles wide, with an estimated three hundred miles of land separating us from the northern end of the sea. Due to the horrible hazards I must admit that I was pretty thoroughly buffaloed and I had quite a few. I've seen enough Aadra today to know that Vishvesh had not exaggerated the dangers. I would not have given a dime of stale beer for the chance to ever see my friends or the outside world again as I stood there beneath that tree that should have been a part of a coal-bed countless ages ago-and looked out across a sea teeming with frightful life. Life that should have been fossil before God conceived of Purush. But then and there, I swore to fight my way as far through this hideous land as conditions would permit I had a heavy rifle, an automatic pistol, and lots of ammo. Twenty more weapons had been added to our arsenal as a result of Vishvesh's account of the enormous predatory animals that decimated Aadra. My biggest threat came from the repulsive reptilia, whose fragile neurological systems allowed them to retain control over their carnivorous urges even after they had died.

But I gave these matters less thought than the abrupt failure of all our preparations. I berated myself bitterly for the stupid weakness that had caused me to be distracted from the primary goal of my flight into premature and pointless exploration. The three hundred miles of Aadraian territory I would have to travel to get to the base of the cliffs where my party was waiting for me seemed to me at that point to be practically insurmountable for a lone traveller unfamiliar with Aadraian life and unaware of everything that lay in front of him. It seemed to me that I would then have to be completely ruled out of any further search for Vishvesh. I could not, however, give up all hope. My obligation seemed obvious to me, and I started travelling north.

The country I travelled through was both wonderful and unusual–I nearly said unearthly-because the flowers, trees, and plants were not from the world I was familiar with. They were bigger, the colours were more vivid, and some of the shapes were practically hideous, they nonetheless added to the romance and enchantment of the surroundings, much as how the enormous cacti make the barren Thar wastelands strangely attractive. The warm, humid air of Aadra-the warm, moist air that lays lethargic upon the breast of this giant mother of life, Nature's mightiest incubator-diffused the light of the sun, which shone over everything else, and it shone enormously, round, and crimson, a monster sun above a monstrous universe.

Life was all around me, in every direction. It leapt from the depths and travelled among the treetops and among the boles. I could hear it in a dense wood at one point as it made big, overlapping circles on the sea's surface. To my right, the murmur of it rising and falling in endless volumes of sound, riven occasionally by a horrifying scream or a tremendous boom that shook the earth; and a strange feeling that a pair of eyes were observing me and soundless feet following me. I don't get anxious or stressed out easily, but the weight of duty on my shoulders made me more careful than usual. To avoid being caught off guard, I frequently turned to the right, left, and back while holding my gun in readiness. I once thought I saw a human figure dart from one cover to another among the numerous critters. I could only dimly make out in the shadows of the wood, but I couldn't be sure.

I avoided the wood's foreboding depths of gloom for the most part, though occasionally I took detours around them. Nevertheless, I frequently had to walk through portions of the woodland that reached the inland sea beach. I always breathed more easily when I returned to open land since the uncouth sounds and hazy sightings of moving objects in the forest gave out such a dark hint of the threat of weird persons and probably even stranger animals.

I had been travelling toward the north for about an hour when, for the a hundredth time, I heard a sound to my right and a little to my rear. I turned and saw an animal running quickly through the forest toward me. I was still convinced that a creature was stalking me and was hiding among the trees and shrubbery to my right and a little to my rear. It made no further attempt to remain hidden; it moved quickly through the underbrush, and I was certain that whatever it was had now mustered the nerve to assault me fearlessly. I realised it wasn't alone before it eventually came into view because a second monster was thrashing through the dense undergrowth a few yards behind him. Evidently, a pair of hunting animals or men were about to assault me in large numbers.

Then, through the final group of swaying ferns, the figure of the dominant beast emerged. I was standing there, guarding the area where I had anticipated it to appear, holding my rifle to my shoulder. If my shock and confusion could be seen in any way, I must have come off as very silly as I lowered my rifle and stared incredulously at the lithe figure of the girl racing quickly in my direction. The biggest cat I've ever seen emerged from the jungle from same area where I had seen her, so I didn't have much time to wait there with my weapon lowered. As she approached, I saw her cast a terrified glance over her shoulder.

I initially mistook the creature for a saber-tooth tiger because it had such a terrifying appearance. However, it was actually quite formidable and could have satisfied even the most ardent thrill seeker. It approached in a grim and terrifying manner, its evil eyes glaring above its protruding jaws, and its lips curled into a terrifying snarl that revealed a mouthful of fearsome teeth. It stopped its hasty advance when it saw me and was now creeping slowly in our direction. The girl, holding a long knife, bravely took position to the left and behind me.

She had called something to me in an unfamiliar language as she ran towards me, and now she was speaking again. I was unable to hear what she had said at the time, but her tone was pleasant, well-modulated, and devoid of any hints of panic.

I waited to take my shot before facing the enormous cat, which I now realised was a huge panther. As shooting any large carnivore in the front is only marginally effective. The fact that the animal wasn't charging, had its head lowered, and had its back exposed gave me a slight advantage. I carefully aimed at the animal's spine at the point where its neck and shoulders meet at a distance of forty yards.

The large animal lifted its head and charged forward at the same time, as though sensing my intention. I quickly adjusted my aim and pulled the trigger, knowing that firing at that sloping forehead would be worse than useless. I was hoping against hope that the soft-nosed bullet and the heavy charge of powder would stall him long enough stopping power to give me time to fire a second shot.

In response to the rifle's, I had the satisfaction of watching the beast leap into the air and perform a full somersault. However, it was back on its feet almost immediately, and in the split second it took to scramble to its feet and regain its bearings, it fully exposed its left side toward me, allowing a second bullet to pierce its heart. It descended once more before rising and coming toward me. One of the amazing characteristics of this strange world is the vitality of its creatures, which is indicative of the primitive nervous system of the old granthic life that has long since disappeared from other parts of the globe.

The beast rolled over and stopped at my feet, stone dead, after I fired a third bullet into it at a distance of three paces. I had then begun to believe that I was doomed. I discovered that my second shot had almost completely severed its heart, yet it had continued to charge at me with ferocity. Had it not been for my third shot, it most likely would have killed me before it finally passed away-

or, as Vishvesh Sudarshana so charmingly puts it, before it realised it was dead.

I turned toward the girl, who was looking at me with obvious admiration and not a little awe, though I must admit that my rifle claimed just as much of her attention as I did. The panther was quite evidently aware that dissolution had overtaken it. She was quite possibly the most amazing animal I have ever seen, and what few of her charms her clothing attempted to conceal, it quite successfully succeeded in highlighting.

Between her right shoulder and elbow was an armlet. A series of armlets covered her left forearm from the elbow to the wrist. When the left arm is raised in guard across the breast or face, these, I later discovered, explained the function of a shield against knife attack.

A wide metal band with a big triangular ornament in the exact centre of her forehead held her thick locks in place. While the metal of all her ornaments was beaten, virgin gold, inlaid in intricate designs with bits of mother-of-pearl and tiny pieces of stone of various colours, this ornament appeared to be a large turquoise. She wore sturdy little sandals on her feet, and a leopard's tail hung from her left shoulder. Her only weapon was a knife. It had an iron blade, grip wrapped in hide with a guard made of three out-bowing strips of flat iron, and a gold knob perched atop the hilt.

In the brief time that we were facing each other, I took all of this in, and noticed another striking aspect of her appearance: she was horribly filthy! Even though her face, limbs, and clothing were stained with mud and sweat, I felt as though I had never seen a creature as perfect and stunning as she was. Her face was equally impossible to describe as her body was. If I were one of these writer-fellows, I would probably describe her features as Grecian, but since I am neither a writer nor a poet, I can describe her features in a way that does her more justice than describing the pronounced sheep like physiognomy of the Greek goddess. No, not even the dirt could conceal the fact that she was breathtakingly beautiful.

She slowly smiled as we stood there staring at each other, parting her symmetrical lips to reveal a row of bright white teeth.

She asked with a rising inflection, "Mahan?"

I replied by pointing to myself and repeating the word after reading in Vishvesh's manuscript that Mahan appeared to denote a higher type of man. She then began what I would assume to be a standard catechism, judging by the inflection, as I could not understand a word she said. The girl kept looking toward the forest the entire time, and at last she touched my arm and pointed there.

When I turned around, I saw a hairy, man-like figure standing and watching us. Soon after, more joined him as they emerged from the jungle, numbering at least twenty in total. They had no clothing on. Although they stood on their feet without touching the ground and had hair covering their bodies, they appeared very ape-like due to their stooped posture, long arms, and somewhat ape-like facial features. With their narrow eyes, flat noses, long upper lips, and protruding yellow fangs, they were not attractive to look at.

"Sood!" the girl exclaimed.

I had read Vishvesh's adventures so many times that I practically knew them by heart. As a result, I was aware that I was seeing the remaining members of that extinct man race the Sood from a long-forgotten era, the speechless man of antiquity.

The girl yelled "Ayya!" at the same time that the Sood started babbling in our direction. As they advanced toward us while baring their fangs, they made strange growling and barking noises.

Despite the fact that they only had nature's weapons-strong muscles and enormous fangs. I knew that these would be more than enough to defeat us if we had no other means of defence, so I drew my pistol and started shooting at the leader. The others turned and fled as he fell like a stone.

The girl grinned slowly once more and approached me, touching my barrel. As she reached out to touch it, I felt a sudden thrill run through me, which I attributed to how long it had been since I had seen a woman of any kind.

She spoke to me in low, ethereal tones, but I was unable to understand her. She then pointed in the direction of the north and turned to leave. Since I was travelling north as well, I decided to follow her. However, even if she had been travelling south, I still would have done so because I was desperate for human company in this world of animals, reptiles, and half-men.

The girl spoke a lot as we walked along, appearing perplexed that I couldn't understand her. When I attempted to speak to her, she responded with a silvery laugh, as if my language was the most archaic thing she had ever heard. She would frequently hold her palm toward me and say, "Mahan!" after failing to communicate with me. She would then touch my breast or arm and scream, "Markat, markat!" I understood what she was getting at because I had read Vishvesh's account and remembered the two words and the unfavourable gesture she used.

She implied that I was a markat, or mute, rather than a Mahan as I had claimed to be. But each time she said this, she laughed again, and her laughter was so contagious that I couldn't help but join in. The fact that she was perplexed by my inability to understand her or make her understand me was only natural, too. From the club-men, the lowest human type in Aadra to speak, to the golden race of Mahans, every tribe's tongue is the same, with the exception of amplified sounds brought on by the increasing scale of evolution.

She, a Mahan, is able to communicate with a Shailtaah and make herself understandable to him as well as to a hatchet-man, spear-man, or archer. It was obvious that her intelligence informed her that I was neither a Kannanaukas nor a Markat, neither an anthropoid ape nor a speechless man. She could only communicate with the Kannanaukass, or apes, the Sood, and myself.

She didn't give up, though, and began to teach me her language. If it weren't for my intense concern for Vishvesh and my Jalayana crewmates, I might have wished the period of instruction went on longer.

Despite how much I enjoy their company, I have never been what one might refer to as a ladies' man. Both in college and since then, I have made friends of both sexes. I believe that I attract a particular kind of girl because I never make love to them. Instead, I leave that to the many others who are infinitely better at it than I could ever hope to be, and I enjoy girls' society in what appear to be more sensible ways, such as dancing, golfing, boating, riding, tennis, and other activities. But in the company of this half-naked little savage, I discovered a new kind of pleasure that was unlike anything I had ever known.

I squealed with delight when she touched me-something I had never done before when in the presence of another woman.

The fact that I am sophisticated enough to know that this is a sign of love and I did not love this filthy little barbarian with her broken, unruly nails and her skin so covered in mud and the green of crushed foliage that it was hard to tell what colour it had originally been left me perplexed. Even though she appeared to be uncouth, she had an innate fineness that dirt could not quite cover up. She had clear eyes, strong, white teeth, a silvery laugh, and a queenly demeanour.

At dusk, we came across a small river that flowed into a sizable bay at the base of low cliffs. As is the case with every journey in this terrifying land thus far our journey too had been fraught with constant danger. I won't bore you with a recounting of the endless series of attacks by the numerous creatures that constantly crossed our path or purposefully pursued us. We were constantly on guard because, to paraphrase, the price of life in this situation is indeed eternal vigilance.

I had made some progress in learning her language and was starting to recognise many of the trees, ferns, grasses, animals, and reptiles by their Aadraian names. I was familiar with the words for the sea, river, cliff, and sky, sun, and cloud. Yes, I was getting along just fine when it occurred to me that I didn't know the name of my companion. I said, "Krishna," to myself and to her while raising my eyebrows in a questioning manner. The girl looked perplexed as she dug her fingers into that mass of hair. I carried out the action twelve times.

Finally, she said, "Krishna," in that resounding, liquid voice. "Krishna!"

I had never given my name much thought before, but when she said it, it suddenly, for the first time in my life, struck me as a very nice name. She then suddenly brightened and tapped her own breast before introducing herself as "Maya!"

"Maya!" She laughed and clapped her hands together when I repeated her name.

We now recognised each other's names, which was a small measure of relief. She was pretty good, Maya! She repeated it, so it appears that she liked mine.

We arrived at the cliffs next to the small river's confluence with the bay and the large inland sea beyond. The cliffs were weathered and rotted, and in one spot a deep hollow extended several feet back beneath the overhanging stone, suggesting a possible place to spend the night. I stopped there to explain to Maya that we would spend the night there because there were loose rocks scattered all around that I could use to construct a barricade across the cave's entrance.

As soon as she understood what I was saying, she nodded in agreement in Aadraian and motioned for me to follow her to the river by touching my rifle. At the bank, she stopped, took off her belt and dagger, putting them to the side, undid the metal leg-band that held the lower edge of her dress, slid it off her left shoulder, and let it fall to the ground around her feet. I was left gasping like a fish out of water as it was done so effortlessly, so quickly, and with such ease. She turned and smiled at me before jumping into the river to take a bath, with me watching over her. She splashed around for five to ten minutes, and when she came to the surface, her skin was smooth, white, and stunning. Without a way to dry herself, she disregarded what would have seemed like a necessity to me and quickly changed into her straightforward but effective costume.

We were only an hour away from darkness when, almost starving, I led the way back a quarter of a mile to a small meadow where we had earlier seen antelope and miniature horses. The rest of the herd fled for the woods after I shot a young buck there, where they encountered a cacophony of horrifying roars as the carnivores took advantage of their panic and leaped among them.

After taking out a hind quarter with my hunting knife, we then went back to the camp. Maya assisted me in gathering a large amount of wood for fire from the nearby fallen trees. I also collected enough loose rock to construct my barricade to protect myself from the terrifying dangers of the approaching night.

I'll never forget the look on Maya's face as she watched me light the kindling next to our campfire with a match. It was the kind of expression that could fill a mortal person with awe as they witnessed the enigmatic actions of divinity. It was clear that Maya had little experience with contemporary fire-making techniques. She had praised my rifle and pistol, but these tiny pieces of wood that, thanks to a magical rub, had lit the campfire were miracles in her eyes.

Maya and I tried to talk once more as the meat roasted over the fire, but despite being brimming with encouragement, gestures, and sounds, the exchange was unremarkably flat. Maya then started working diligently to teach me her language. She started off, as I later discovered, using the most basic form of speech used by the Shailtaah, which is known to Aadra or, for that matter, the entire world. Even though my instructor's inability to speak my language was a significant disadvantage for her, she performed remarkably well and showed that she had a high level of ingenuity and intelligence. I found it to be far from difficult.

After dinner, I added more wood to the pile to rekindle the fire in front of our barricade because I thought it would be the best defence against carnivores. Maya and I then sat down in front of the fire to continue the lesson as the strange and amazing sounds of the Aadraian night erupted all around us: the howling and barking of a wolverine, the roaring of tigers, panthers, and lions.

I was so focused on my lesson and my teacher that many times I was deaf to what, at another time, would have filled me with awe, despite the fact that the voice of this choir-terrible rose and fell from far and near in all directions, at times reaching such a tremendous volume of sound that the earth shook to it. Every sense and organ in my body was completely occupied by the attractive voice and face of the girl as she eagerly leaned towards me to correct my pronunciation of a word or explain its meaning to me. The firelight glistened on the smooth firmness of her flawless skin, glistened from her white teeth and from her golden jewellery, and highlighted her animated features and sparkling eyes. It also highlighted the graceful motions of her gesturing arms and hands. Even so, I still learned a lot that evening, even though some of it had nothing to do with learning a new language. I'm afraid that I was frequently more preoccupied with admiration of this beautiful animal than with a desire for knowledge.

I thought I detected a hint of Maya's desire for me to speak Aadraian as quickly as possible—a quality that is uniquely feminine and has been passed down through the ages from the first lady of the world. I was certain that Maya wanted me to speak in her language so that she could satisfy a curiosity about me that was causing her to feel like she might burst. She was just your typical animated question mark. She burbled with questions that would never be answered unless I picked up her language.

Her little tongue raced with time, her eyes sparkled with excitement, and her hand flew in expressive gestures, but to no avail. The result was that Maya would become so enraged that she would clench her little fists and beat me on the breast as hard as she could, and then she would sink back laughing as the humour of the situation captured her. I could speak perfectly Aadraian, but my vocabulary was only tantalising; it did not lend itself well to a very general conversation.

She was attempting to teach me some verbs by performing the actions while repeating the correct word. We had become completely absorbed, paying no attention to events outside of our cave, when Maya abruptly stopped and cried, "Ayya!" Considering that she had been trying to teach me that it meant stop, when she simultaneously cried Ayya and stopped, I briefly believed that this was part of my lesson and temporarily forgot that Ayya also meant beware.

As a result, I repeated the word after her. However, when I noticed the look in her eyes as they were directed past me and her finger pointing in the direction of the cave's entrance, I quickly turned around and saw a hideous face at the tiny opening leading out into the night. It was the ferocious and snarling face of an enormous bear. I've hunted silvertips in the White Mountains of Himalayas, and I considered them to be among the biggest and toughest quarry. However, after seeing this terrifying animal's head, I concluded that even the biggest grizzly bear I've ever seen would be dwarfed by the size of a huge dog.

Our fire was located right inside the cave, and the smoke rose from it through the cracks in the rocks I had stacked so that they curved inward toward the top cliff. The entrance we needed to use to leave was covered with a few sizable pieces, but they did not completely block it. No large animal could enter through the openings that were left open as a result. However, I had relied on our fire the most because I believed that none of the dangerous nocturnal predators would approach the flames. I was clearly mistaken in thinking so, as the large bear was standing just a foot away from the flames that were dying out as I had been preoccupied with my lesson and my teacher that I had forgotten to replenish them.

Maya pointed to my rifle while brandishing her useless little knife. She spoke in a calm, level voice that was completely devoid of any signs of anxiety or panic. I was aware that she was urging me to shoot the beast, but I only wanted to do so as a last resort because I was confident that even my heavy bullets would only aggravate him further, which would make it much easier for him to force his way into our cave.

Rather than firing, I added more wood to the fire, and as the smoke and blaze rose in the beast's face, it backed away while growling terribly. However, I could still make out two unsightly points of light blazing in the outer darkness, and I could still hear the beast's growls rumbling tremendously outside. The creature watched the entrance to our flimsy sanctuary for a while as I futilely tried to come up with a strategy for defence or escape. I was fully aware that if the bear made a determined attempt to approach us, the rocks I had piled as a defence would collapse around his enormous shoulders like a house of cards, and he could then approach us directly.

Maya begged me to shoot the beast, but I knew that the likelihood that I could do so with a single shot was extremely remote while the possibility that I would only enrage it was real and present. I waited for what felt like an eternity, watching those devilish points of fire glaring balefully at us and listening to the ever-increasing volume of those seismic growls which seemed to be coming from nowhere.

It didn't matter how much wood I added to the fire, even though Maya and I were on the verge of roasting; the mighty engine of destruction kept going until the hideous face yawed its fanged yawn directly into the barrier's opening. It stood like this for a short while before withdrawing its head. I exhaled a sigh of relief because the thing had changed its mind and was now looking for easier to capture prey. The fire was too much for it, but my happiness was fleeting, and I felt my heart sink once more when I saw a large paw-one that was the size of a large dishpan-insinuated into the opening seconds later. The paw gently tugged and pulled on the large rock that partially blocked the entrance before very deliberately pulling it outward to one side. Once more, the head entered the cavern, but the large shoulders were still unable to fit through the gap. Maya drew nearer until her shoulder touched mine, and although she didn't show any other signs of fear, I thought I noticed a slight tremble run through her body.

Unintentionally, I wrapped my left arm around her and briefly drew her close to me. I must admit that I swooned once more at contact with her, even in the face of death, I released her and threw my rifle to my shoulder because, at last, I had come to the realisation that there was nothing more to be gained by waiting. The creature was coming toward us, and our only chance was to fire as many shots into it as I could. Already having removed a second rock, it was about to force its enormous bulk through the gap that it had created.

I then carefully aimed between its eyes, closing my right fingers evenly and firmly on the stock's trivial while pulling my trigger finger back with a strong hand motion. It was impossible for the bullet to miss its target! I forced myself not to breathe so as not to veer the muzzle even slightly. On the target range, I was as calm and steady as I had ever been, and I was fully anticipating a perfect hit; I knew I could not miss. The hammer then fell on an unusable cartridge as the bear charged forward toward me. A perfectly hellish roar erupted almost simultaneously from somewhere, and the bear quickly retreated from the cave after uttering a series of growls that far exceeded anything he had previously attempted in volume and ferocity.

For a brief moment, I was unable to comprehend what had happened to cause this sudden retreat when his prey was almost in his grasp. He couldn't possibly believe that a harmless click of the hammer had scared him. We didn't have to wait long, though, before we could at least speculate as to what had caused the distraction. Outside, we could hear mingled growls and roars as well as the sound of massive bodies flailing about until the ground trembled.

The bear was now engaged in a fierce battle for dominance after being attacked in the back by another powerful animal. The battle continued for the better part of an hour, with occasional breaks during which we could hear the combatants' laboured breathing, until the sounds of combat gradually decreased and then eventually vanished entirely. We sat and waited for the winner of the battle to come and claim his reward; however, despite sitting for a considerable amount of time with our eyes glued to the opening, we saw no sign of any beast. Maya suggested, in sign and broken words, to move the fire directly to the cave entrance.

Maya finally agreed to lay down because I knew she needed to sleep, and I remained vigilant until nearly morning. Then, the girl woke up and insisted that I get some rest. She wouldn't accept no for an answer, and dragged me down while laughingly threatening me with her razor blade.

***

*

When I woke up, it was daytime, and I discovered Maya roasting a sizable piece of antelope meat while crouching before a fine bed of coals. The experience from the previous night had all but destroyed my happiness and hope, but the sight of the new day and the mouth-watering aroma of the cooking meat restored them. Perhaps it was the slender figure of the cheerful-faced girl. Her perfect grin as she looked up at me and dimpling with apparent happiness was the cutest thing I had ever seen. I remember that this was the first time I regretted that she was so much more evolved than I was and only a tiny bit of an untrained savage.

A large saber-tooth tiger, with its fine coat and flesh torn to ribbons, lay dead just a few paces from our cave, and next to it was the carcass of a large cave bear. She then motioned for me to follow her outside, where she pointed to the scene that had led to our escape from the bear. It was, to put it mildly, unusual to have one's life saved by a saber-tooth tiger in the twentieth century, but it had happened, and I could see the evidence of it right in front of me.

The great carnivora of Aadra are so enormous that they must constantly eat in order to maintain their enormous thews. As a result, they will consume the meat of any other animal and attack anything that comes within their range, regardless of how powerful the prey may be. Later observation led me to the conclusion that larger carnivorous reptiles, such as the cave bear, cave lion, and saber-tooth tiger, typically make two kills per day: one in the morning and one after dark. I mention this because it merits the attention of Granthgyata and naturalists. They immediately eat the entire carcass before lying down and sleeping for a while.

Luckily, they are relatively rare; otherwise, Aadra would be devoid of all life. Because of their extreme voracity, other forms of life are able to survive because even during the mating season, large males frequently devour their own mates, and both sexes occasionally eat their young. It completely baffles me how the human and semi human races have survived here for countless of years under the existing conditions.

Maya and I departed again for our northward journey after breakfast. We had only travelled a short distance when we came under attack from several apelike creatures carrying clubs. They appeared to be on a slightly higher than the Sood. They were Shailtaah, or clubmen, according to Maya. One of them was killed by a revolver shot, and the others scattered yet we continued to face the threat of an attack for the rest of the day, up until we entered the Shailatiya, or hatchet-men, country. These people appeared less eager to destroy us and were less hairy and more resembled men. They were curious and followed us for a distance while closely inspecting us.

They called out to us, and Maya responded. However, her responses did not seem to appease them, and they eventually started to act threateningly toward us. I believe they were about to attack us when a small deer that had been hiding in some low bush suddenly broke cover and ran across from our front. It was getting close to one o' clock. I pulled out my gun and fired one round, stopping the creature in its tracks. The Shailtaah experienced an electrical reaction. They immediately gave up any thoughts of attacking us and fled towards the forest that was lining our route. We spent that night in the Shailatiya region by a small stream. We discovered a small cave in the rock bank that was so obscured that only luck could lead a predator to it.

After eating some of the deer meat and fruit that Maya had collected, we crept into the tiny opening and I erected a sturdy barricade with the sticks and stones I had specifically collected for the task. Without swimming or wading through the stream, nothing could get to us, and I felt completely safe from attack. Our accommodations were fairly small. We struggled to fit together in the confined flooring and low ceiling but had to make the most of the situation as we were both extremely exhausted. The sense of security was so strong that I'm positive I fell asleep as soon as I stretched out next to Maya.

We made frustratingly slow progress over the next three days, probably covering bare ten miles. We were forced to spend hours at a time in hiding from one or more of the large animals that constantly threatened us due to the country's horrifyingly savage conditions. Numerous different carnivores had come out, reptiles were scarce but the one's we did encounter were gigantic.

I will never forget one particularly large specimen that we came across at the edge of the large sea as it was grazing on some water reeds. At its highest point, the rump, it was well over twelve feet tall. With its incredibly long tail and neck, it was between 75 and 100 feet long. Although its body was unarmored and its head was absurdly small, its enormous bulk gave it a very intimidating appearance.

My knowledge of Aadraian culture led me to believe that the enormous creature would only need to see us in order to attack us, so I raised my rifle and withdrew toward some brush that provided cover. Maya, however, only laughed and grabbed a stick before running toward the enormous creature while yelling.

The animal looked around aimlessly looking for the source of the disturbance with its tiny head raised high upon its long neck. When the tiny Maya was finally spotted by its eyes, she threw the stick at him. The enormous creature shuffled into the water and let out a cry that was somewhat akin to a sheep's bleat. It quickly immersed. I realised that I had observed nothing less than a diplodocus of the Jurassic as I slowly recalled my college studies and Granth readings from Vishvesh's textbooks, but how incredibly different the real, live thing was from the shoddy refurbishments of Hatcher and Holland! I mistakenly believed the diplodocus to be a land animal, but it appears that it is only partially amphibious. Since my first sighting, I have seen several, and in each instance the creature fled to the sea for cover as soon as it was startled. It had no defensive weapons other than its enormous tail, but it can deliver such a powerful blow with this limb that it can leave even a giant cave bear for stunned, broken and dead.

It is one of the few creatures in Aadra to which the description "stupid, simple, gentle beast" might even remotely apply.

We had to sleep on thick tree branches for three continuous nights due to lack of any cavernous regions. Atleast here, we were safe from attacks from large land carnivora, but smaller flying reptiles, snakes, leopards, and panthers were a constant threat-even though they were nowhere near as terrifying as the enormous animals that roamed the earth's surface.

Maya and I were able to speak quite fluently by the end of the third day, which was a huge relief for both of us but especially for Maya. She now only asked questions whenever I would let her, which wasn't very often because I had a lot of my own to ask since our survival was largely dependent on how quickly I could learn about the geography and customs of Aadra.

I had a great time talking to her and answering her questions because she was so naive and in awe of everything, I told her about the world outside of Aadra's high walls. She never once seemed to doubt me, no matter how amazing my claims must have seemed, and they undoubtedly made Maya wonder because she had never imagined that anything existed outside of Aadra and the life she knew.

Despite the fact that many of her questions lacked artistic flair, they nonetheless revealed a sharp intellect and a cunningness that seemed far beyond her years or her experience. Overall, I thought my little savage was a very interesting and likeable person, and I frequently expressed gratitude to fate for bringing us together. She taught me a lot about Aadra, but the mystery that had perplexed Vishvesh Sudarshana complete lack of young among the ape, semi human, and human races-with which both he and I had come into contact on opposite shores of the inland sea still remained unanswered. Maya made an effort to explain the situation to me, but it was clear that she was having trouble understanding why something so normal should require explanation. She explained to me that while some Mahans were infants-she herself had once been one—the majority of her people "came up," as he put it, "aage badho," or literally, "from the beginning." And as they all did when they used that phrase, she would wave broadly toward the south.

"My mother kept me hidden for long," she said, leaning very close to me and speaking into my ear while casting anxious glances in all directions, mainly upward, "lest the Bhootnath, passing through the air by night, should come and take me away to Haveli." As she said the word, the girl trembled. I pressed her for more information, but she was so terrified when she spoke of the Bhootnath and their place of residence, Haveli, that I eventually gave up. Nevertheless, I did learn that the Bhootnath only kidnapped female babies and occasionally Mahans women who had "come from the start."

I had the impression that the Bhootnaths were imaginary beings-the demons or gods of her race, omniscient and omnipresent. It was all very mysterious and incomprehensible.

This gave me reason to believe that the Mahans were religious, and further probing revealed that this was indeed the case. Maya spoke reverently of the god of heat and life, Agni. She informed me that they revered Agni in a variety of guises, including as fire, the sun, and other tangible objects that symbolised warmth and procreation.

Maya would draw an isosceles swastik with her forefinger in front of her whenever I built a fire, and she also did it in the morning when she first saw the sun. When we started talking and she briefly explained some of her religious superstitions, I realised that she was making the swastik sign, which is similar to how a German make theirs.

At first, I had not associated her act with anything in particular. The swastik's short side was always on top. She showed me the decorations on her golden armlets, the dagger's knob, and the band that encircled her right leg above the knee as she explained everything to me. Each decoration was partially made up of isosceles swastiks, and when she explained the significance of this particular geometric shape, I immediately understood how appropriate it was.

We had now arrived in the homeland of the Aadra spearmen known as the Gorkha. I was eager to see them because Vishvesh had said in his account that they were comparable to the so-called human race of the Initial Tretha. I saw them, so I wasn't disappointed either. Due to the fact that we had reached a line of cliffs running east and west and had literally battled our way through cordons of wild animals for two days after leaving the Shailatiya country, we decided to set up camp a little earlier than usual.

Both of us were extremely exhausted, and the sight of these caverns—many of which could be easily fortified- decided us to stop until the next morning. After only a brief period of exploration, we located a cavern high up the cliff face that seemed perfect for our needs. The entrance was so small that we had to lie down and wriggle through it in order to enter, but the interior was large and had high ceilings. It opened onto a small ledge where we could build our cookfire. I lit a faggot and peered around, but all I could see was that the chamber continued back into the ledge.

I left Maya in the cave and set down my rifle, pistol, and bulky ammunition belt as I descended to gather firewood. We already had fresh water, meat, and fruit that we had just before arriving at the cliffs. We only needed fuel hence, I refused to let Maya come with me and let her conserve her strength. The poor girl was exhausted, but I know that she would have followed me until the very end because she was so devoted to me.

She was the best friend, anyone could have, and sometimes I wished she was from my world and other times, I was relieved that she wasn't because I would have fallen in love with her without a doubt. As it stood, we had a great deal of respect for one another but no softer feelings as we travelled together like two boys. I was forced to enter the wood some two hundred yards away because there wasn't much wood close to the base of the cliffs. I now understand how foolish it was for me to enter a place like Aadra, which is rife with danger and death. However, every man possesses a certain amount of foolishness, and whatever portion of it I possess must have been dominant that day, as the truth is that I entered those woods completely defenceless, and I paid the price, as people typically do for their transgressions.

With my head bowed and eyes on the ground, I combed the underbrush for potential firewood when all of a sudden I felt a heavy weight fall upon me. I fought to get to my knees and grabbed my attacker, a large, snakeskin-covered man who was otherwise naked with his head hanging to his knees. The man was armed with a hatchet, a stone knife, and a spear with stone shoes. He had several feathers in his black hair that were grey in colour. As we struggled back and forth, I was beginning to gain the upper hand when a number of his friends rushed up and dominated me.

They carefully examined me before tying long raw hide thongs around my hands behind me. Most of them, in my opinion, were handsome examples of manhood. Some of them were hairy and resembled the Shailatiya, but the majority had large heads and not unattractive features. They didn't have as much in common with apes as the Shailatiya, Shailtaah, and Sood did. They did not immediately kill me as I had anticipated. Instead, they questioned me, but it was clear they did not buy my story because they laughed and scoffed at it.

They cried, "The Mahans have driven you out." "You'll pass away if you return to them. You will perish if you don't leave now. We will kill you, but first we will dance-the dance of death-and you will dance with us."

It was quite consoling to hear! However, I took heart in the knowledge that I would not be put to death right away. They guided me toward the cliffs, and as we got closer, I looked up and thought I could see Maya's bright eyes watching over us from our lofty cave. However, she didn't make any moves to let me know if she saw me, so we continued on and rounded the end of the cliffs before moving along its opposite face until we reached an area that was literally honeycombed with caves.

Numerous tribe members could be seen everywhere, both on the ground and swarming the ledges in front of the entrances. Despite the fact that there were many women but no babies or young children, I did notice that the females' breasts were more developed than those of the Shailtaah, Shailatiya, Sood or apes. In reality, the female breast among the lower orders of Aadraian specie is merely a rudimentary organ, barely suggested in the apes and Sood, and only slightly more defined in the Shailtaah and Shailatiya, though always increasing to the point where it is found about half developed in the females of the spear-men. However, there was never any sign that the females had suckled young, and there were no children among them. The women varied in attractiveness. There were some who strongly resembled the Shailatiya type, but there were also some who were genuinely handsome and had completely hairless bodies. All had heavy, symmetrical figures. All Sood have beards, but among the Shailtaah, the beard is absent in the female population.

The Gorkha men don't have a beard, whereas the Shailatiya men do, and their women have very little hair on their bodies.

The tribe members were very interested in me, particularly my clothing, which was obviously something they had never seen before. Although some of them struck me and pulled and hauled me, for the most part they were not particularly brutal. The only ones who mistreated me were the hairier ones, who most resembled the Shailatiya. Finally, my captors took me into a large cave with a fire burning at its mouth. The air was filled with the foul smell of decaying flesh and human remains, and the floor was covered in garbage, including numerous animal bones. Here, they fed me while letting go of my arms, and I consumed a stew that might have been made of snakes based on how many of the long, round pieces of meat reminded me so strongly of them.

After the meal was finished, they led me deep inside the cavern, lighting it with torches inserted into various cracks. It was then that I discovered, to my surprise, that the walls were covered in paintings and etchings. Aurochs, red deer, saber-tooth tigers, cave bears, hyaenadons, and many other members of the Aadra fauna were painted or scratched on the rock surface. The colours used were typically four shades of brown. They were frequently superimposed on top of one another to the point where it took close inspection to identify the different outlines. Vishvesh's comparisons between these people and the extinct Rachetaas, whose ancient art is still preserved in the caverns of Ajanta and Ellora, were strengthened by the fact that they all displayed a rather remarkable aptitude for delineation. The Gorkha, however, did not use a bow and arrow, setting them apart from their extinct forebears or offspring from Western India in this regard.

If any of my friends have the chance to read about my adventures on Swaraj Dweep, I sincerely hope they won't find these diversionary tales to be boring. If they do, I can only explain that I am writing my memoirs for my own edification and am thus including those things that particularly interested me at the time. While I don't apologise for my philosophical pontification, I humbly explain to them that they are witnessing the gropings of a finite mind after the infinite, the search for explanations of the inexplicable. I have no desire for the general public to ever have access to these pages, but it is possible that my friends and some savants who are interested might.

My captors ordered me to stop in a distant corner of the cavern. My hands and feet were both held down once more. Even though they were unable to believe or even comprehend the truth of my origin and the circumstances of my arrival in Aadra, I was extremely grateful that the marked similarity between the various tribal tongues of Aadra enabled us to understand each other perfectly while they interrogated me. They eventually left me, saying that they would return for me before the dance of death the following morning. I realised before they left with their torches that I had not been taken to the farthest end of the cavern because a dim corridor led from my cell to the interior of the ledge.

I couldn't help but be in awe of the massive size of underground grotto. I had already travelled several hundred yards of it, and there were numerous points where other corridors split off. I was filled with dread at the thought that the more remote passages might be home to ferocious animals with different entry and exit points than the Gorkha because the entire cliff must be honeycombed with apartments and passages, of which this community only occupied a relatively small portion.

I like to think that I don't get hysterically anxious, but I have to admit that the circumstances I had found myself in, I felt a little uneasy. However, the future held fewer dreads for me than the present, and I challenge any rational person to tell me that it is not terrifying to lie bound hand and foot in the intense blackness of a vast cave inhabited by unknown dangers in a region overrun by hideous beasts and fierce reptiles. Some silent-footed predator might detect my scent from where they were hiding in a nearby passage at any time, possibly even right now, and sneak up on me.

I craned my neck around as I searched through the pitch-blackness for the two blazing spots of hatred that would, in my mind, signal the arrival of my executioner. The images in my overworked mind were so vivid that I broke out in a cold sweat, convinced that a beast was standing right in front of me. However, the hours passed without a sound breaking the cavern's eerie silence.

Many of my life's experiences—including a huge parade of friends and occasions that would be permanently erased the following day—passed before my mental vision during that seemingly endless time. I berated myself for the stupid decision that had separated me from the search team that was so dependent on me, and I pondered whether or not they had made any progress. Were they still waiting for me to return beyond the barrier cliffs? Or had they managed to get inside Aadra? I had a feeling that it could be the case as latter the party did not consist of men who were easily distracted from their goals. It was highly likely that they were already looking for me, but I had my doubts about whether they would ever turn up anything. I had long since come to the conclusion that it was beyond human capability to circumnavigate the inland sea of Aadra in the face of the numerous dangers that lurked in every corner of this world during both day and night. Since I had long since given up on ever making it to the point where I had made my entry into the country, I was now completely convinced that our entire expedition had been worse than pointless before it had even been thought of. Vishvesh J. Sudarshana and his wife could not possibly have survived throughout all of these long months, and neither could Agnivesh and his crew of sailors still be alive.

However, long before that, my bones would be added to the debris on the floor of this great cavern. If my party's superior force and equipment had allowed them to circle the northern end of the sea, they might have found the broken wreck of my plane hanging in the large tree to the south. The idea of a flawless girl, clear-eyed, strong, straight, and beautiful, with the carriage of a queen and the supple, undulating grace of a leopard, moved through all of my thoughts, both realistic and fantastical. The fate of this little barbarian stranger, for whom, I had convinced myself repeatedly, I felt no greater sentiment than passing friendship for a fellow-wayfarer in this land of horrors, seemed more important to me than the fate of my friends, even though I loved them.

However, I was so concerned and anxious about her and her future that I eventually forgot about my own situation, despite my intermittent attempts to break free of my bonds. I was more concerned that I would get to her protection quickly than that I would avoid the fate that was predetermined for me. A distinct and unmistakable sound of padded feet moving stealthily in my direction came from the dark corridor further toward the centre of the cliff while I was thus occupied and had temporarily forgotten my concerns about scavenging animals. The voice startled me into tense silence.

I don't think I've ever felt such extreme horror as I did when I realised that I would have to lie bound and defenceless while some hideous predator crept up on me to devour me in the pitch-black Gorkha pits of Aadra. My skin crawled, and I could feel it crawling, and I reeked with cold sweat. I can't remember if I've ever been more cowardly, but it wasn't out of fear of dying because I had long since accepted that I was lost. A few days in Aadra should have made anyone realise how meaningless life is.

It's everywhere-in the air, on land, and in the waters—and it's constantly being eaten by some other kind of life. The cheapest thing in Aadra is life, which is also true for the earth and, most likely, for all of creation. No, I wasn't afraid of dying; in fact, I prayed for death in order to be freed from the terrifying portion of my remaining life-the agonising wait for that terrifying beast to attack me.

It got to the point where I could hear it breathing. It touched me, and then leaped back as if I had just appeared out of nowhere. No sound broke the eerie silence of the cave for extended periods of time. After that, I heard the creature moved closer to me, and it once more touched me. This time, I felt what felt like a hairless hand move over my face and down until it touched the collar of my flannel shirt. Then, quietly but with much pent-up emotion, a voice cried out, "Krishna!"

So strong was the reaction that I believe I almost passed out. I managed to say, "Maya!" Can it be you, Maya, my girl?

She cried out in a trembling little voice, "Oh, Krishna!" and threw herself onto me while sobbing softly. I had no idea Maya was capable of crying.

She told me that she had followed the Gorkha until they took me into the cave, which she had seen was on the opposite side of the cliff from ours, she knew that she could do nothing for me until the Gorkha fell asleep. She had seen them coming out of the forest with me. She had to struggle to get there after being pursued and nearly attacked by a cave lion. I shook at the danger she had taken.

She planned to approach the cave where I was trapped and rescue me after midnight, when the majority of the carnivora would have made their kills. She explained that she intended to frighten the Gorkha with my rifle and pistol–both of which she assured me she could use after having observed me so frequently–and force them to give me up. Little girl is brave! She would have willingly risked her life to save me. But shortly after entering our cave, she heard voices coming from a distance and immediately deduced that we had only discovered a different entrance to the caves that the Gorkha lived in on the opposite side of the cliff. Then, having no other means of guidance than her incredible sense of direction, she had set out through those winding passages and made her way to where I was lying in complete darkness.

She had to move with extreme caution lest she fall into a dark abyss, and in reality, she had encountered three sheer drops and had to take the most terrifying risks to get past them. Even now, when I think about what this girl endured for my benefit, I shudder. She increased her risk by putting herself in danger by carrying the awkwardly long rifle, arms and ammunitions that she wasn't used to.

I could have bowed down and given her a reverent, grateful kiss, and I'm not ashamed to say that's exactly what I did after being released from my bonds and learning about her struggles. Little Maya, be brave! Wonder-girl from a distant, unimaginable past! She had never received a kiss before, but she leaned forward in the dark and placed her own lips on my forehead, indicating that she understood the significance of the new caress. I suddenly had the urge to grab her, pull her close to my chest, and kiss her hot young lips passionately, but I restrained myself because I knew I didn't love her, and kissing her that way would have been a grave injustice to her who had sacrificed her life for mine.

No, Maya should be just as safe with me as she would be with her own mother, if she had one, which I had my doubts about even though she told me her mother had once hidden her when she was a baby. I had started to wonder if Aadra even had mothers like the ones we are accustomed to!

No word exists in the Pahadi that corresponds to our word mother. They point toward the south and mention prajananand aarambh, which translate to "reproduction and from the beginning," but no one has a mom. We eventually arrived at what we believed to be our cave, only to discover that it wasn't, and then we realised that we were lost in the vast labyrinth of cavern . We tried to go back where we had come from by retracing our steps, but all that happened was that we became even more disoriented. Maya was shocked, but not so much by our situation as by the fact that she had failed to use the wonderful sense she shared with the majority of other

Aadraian creatures in order to move from place to place without a compass or other sort of manual.

We moved slowly hand in hand as we looked for a way out of the great cliff, aware that with every step we might be making our way deeper into its heart or circling aimlessly in a wandering that could only lead to death. the darkness! It was so miserable that it was almost palpable. We couldn't afford to waste any of the matches I had, so I struck one in some of the trickier spots. Nevertheless, we had to move slowly and did our best to stay in one general direction in the hopes that it would eventually take us to a doorway leading to the outside planet. When I lit some matches, I discovered that there were no paintings on the walls, no evidence that people had descended this far into the cliff, and no other animal spoor of any kind.

It would have been difficult to estimate how much time we spent stumbling through those gloomy passageways, scaling steep hills, navigating around the edges of bottomless pits, never knowing when we might fall into some abyss, and constantly being plagued by the constant fear of starvation and thirst-related death. Even though it was challenging, I still understood that it could have been much worse if I hadn't had the brave, conscientious, and devoted little Maya by my side. She must have been exhausted, hungry, and thirsty, but she never wavered in her cheer.

If she died of hunger, at least she would die with me, and she was quite content that such should be her end, she said when I asked if she was afraid or not. Here, the Bhootnath could not get her, she said. At the time, I explained her behaviour as being similar to a dog's devotion to a new master who had treated her well. I'll swear under penalty of perjury that I didn't think it was anything so much.

I was unable to determine how long we had been trapped inside the cliff, and I still don't know. We grew extremely hungry and tired; the hours dragged; we slept at least twice; after which, we got up and stumbled along, getting weaker and weaker each time. There were periods of time when the upward trend of the corridor was constant. When we were as exhausted as we were at the time, it was heartbreaking work, but we clung tenaciously to it. We stumbled, fell, and sank due to a physical inability to keep our feet, but we always managed to get back up and continue. We had initially avoided getting separated by walking hand in hand whenever possible.

Later, when I noticed that Maya was deteriorating quickly, we walked side by side with me holding an arm around her abdomen. I still carried a heavy load of weapons, but now that the rifle was strapped to my back, my hands were free. When I too began to exhibit undeniable signs of exhaustion, Maya advised that I put down my weapons and ammunition; however, I refused, explaining that crossing Aadra without them would mean certain death, I might as well take the chance of dying here in the cave with them since there was a second possibility that we might find our way to freedom.

Maya was able to walk again at some point, and at that point I picked her up and carried her. She pleaded with me to leave her, telling me that if I found a way out, I could return and get her. However, she knew-and she knew that I knew-that if I did leave her, there was no way I would ever be able to find her again. Still, she persisted. I could hardly move more than a dozen steps at a time before I had to sit down and relax for three to eight minutes.

I'm not sure what drove me forward and kept me going in the face of a firm conviction that my efforts were completely in vain. Even though I considered Maya and I to be close to dead, I continued to drag myself along until I was only able to move forward by crawling a few inches at a time. She pleaded to me to leave her and save myself in a soft voice that was now almost inaudible due to weakness still she seemed to be thinking only of me. No matter how much I might have wanted to, I couldn't have left her there alone. However, the truth was that I didn't want to leave her. The words that came out of my mouth to her then were very easy and natural. With death so close by, I doubt people would have been very inclined to heroics, so it couldn't very well have been otherwise. We were resting against a rocky wall, and Maya was leaning against me, her head on my chest. "I would rather not get out at all, Maya," I said to her. She leaned in closer to me and gave my arm a weak caress with one hand, but she said nothing because it wasn't essential.

After our brief break we resumed our completely hopeless journey. However, I soon realised that I was losing strength, and eventually I had to admit defeat. I told Maya, "I've come as far as I can; it's pointless. Perhaps if I sleep, I can continue later. "However, I was aware that it was untrue and that the end was drawing near. Maya replied, "Yes, sleep." We were going to bed together, forever!

As I lay on the hard floor, she snuck up behind me and rested her head on my arm. I must have passed out almost instantly because I don't remember anything after I pulled her close until our lips touched before saying, "Good-bye!" I later awoke from a restless dream in which I dreamed that I was drowning to find the cave lit by what appeared to be diffused daylight and a tiny trickle of water running down the corridor and forming a puddle in the small depression in which it chanced to fall.

I quickly turned to look at Maya out of concern for what the light might reveal, but she was still breathing, albeit very softly. Then, after looking around for an explanation of the light, I quickly realised that it was coming from a bend in the corridor just ahead of us, at the top of a steep incline. Immediately, I realised that Maya and I had almost accidentally found the portal of salvation during night. We might have been irreparably lost and may still be lost if fate had led us a few extra yards up one of the corridors that split off from ours just ahead of us, but at least we would have been able to pass through outside of the terrifying darkness of this terrible cave. When I tried to stand up, I discovered that sleep had restored some of my strength. I was further revived when I tasted the water. Maya did not respond to my gentle shoulder shake, so I gathered a few drops of water in my cupped hand and gently dripped them on her lips. She was revived by this, and she raised her eyes and grinned when she saw me.

She questioned, "What happened? Where are we now?

"I retorted, "We are at the end of the corridor, and daylight is streaming in from outside just ahead. Maya, you've saved us!"

She stood up and looked around before crying in a very . Of course, it was the response, and she was also extremely frail at the time. She finally got to her feet with my assistance after I calmed her down as much as I could, as she as well as I had found a small amount of relief in naps. Together, we stumbled up the hill toward the light. At the first bend, we saw a gap ahead of us and a leaden sky beyond. From the leaden sky, a drizzling rain was pouring down, creating the small, trickling stream that had provided us with water when we most needed it.

The rain was warmer than the atmosphere in those dim passages. The cave had been damp and cold, but as we crawled through the aperture, the muggy warmth of the Aadraian air caressed and confronted us. We now had water and warmth, and I was confident that Aadra would soon provide us with meat or fruit. However, when we got to a point where we could look around, we discovered that we were on top of a cliff, where there didn't seem to be much reason to expect quarry. There were trees, though, and we soon discovered edible fruits among them that we then used to break our lengthy fast.

***

*

We rested and recovered for two days atop the cliff. We were able to eat some small quarry and quench our thirst with the help of the small pools of rainwater. A few hours after we emerged from the cave, the sun came out, and in its warmth, we quickly shed the melancholy that our recent experiences had forced to deal upon us. On the third day's morning, we started looking for a way to get to the valley. In the distance, beyond and close to the base of the formidable barrier-cliffs, we could see a sizable group of Gorkha warriors travelling north for a hunt. Below us, to the north, we could make out the Gorkha women lying in the shallow waters of a large pool. We enjoyed a beautiful view from our perch atop a cliff. We could faintly make out the farther shore of the inland sea to the west, and to the southwest, the large southern island stood out visibly in front of us.

It would have been easily visible from our altitude and in a clearer atmosphere, but Aadra's humid climate causes distant objects to appear blurry and hazy. Maya also claimed that the mainland to the east of Haveli was her territory-the Mahan's land. She indicated the cliffs at its southern border, which serve as the country of the

Pahadi—the archers—south of which is the frontier. Now all that remained for us to do was cross the remaining Gorkha and Pahadi territory in order to enter the boundaries of her country. However, doing so required travelling through 38 miles of hostile territory that was home to numerous terrifying creatures that were likely beyond my capacity to imagine. At that point, I would have given anything for my plane because it would have brought us within twenty minutes of Maya's territory.

We eventually located a spot where we could hang off the edge of the cliff and onto a small ledge that appeared to have once been a quarry path leading to the valley, though it had apparently been abandoned for some time. The drop was significant and the ledge terrifyingly narrow, with a sheer frightful drop below down to the rocks at the base of the cliff; I freely admit that my hair stood on their end during the process, but with Maya there to hold and support me, I made it through , and then we established off down the path towards the valley. Although there were a few more difficult spots, overall it was a simple descent and we arrived at the highest Gorkha caves without further incident. We moved more slowly in this area out of fear that a tribesman would ambush us.

Before being accosted, we must have advanced through about half of the Gorkha cave levels. A huge man then stepped out in front of me and blocked our progress.

He asked, "Who are you," and I answered that he should know because he was one of the people who had led me back into the cave and bound me the night I had been kidnapped. His eyes left me and turned to Maya. He was the highest class of Aadraian I had yet seen, with the exception of Maya, of course. He had a handsome appearance, clear, intelligent eyes, a good forehead, and a superb physique.

"You are a true Mahan, but this man is made from a different mould, he told Maya. He has a Mahan face, but neither the Mahans nor the Aadra are represented in his weapons or the strange skins he sports on his body.

Who is he?"

He is Krishna, Maya said succinctly.

The Gorkha stated quite honestly, playing with his spear in a very suggestive manner, "There is no such people."

I thought it best to propitiate him if I could, both out of necessity to conserve ammunition and to avoid the loud alarm of a shot which might bring other Gorkha warriors upon us. "My name is Krishna, and I am from a country beyond Aadra," I said. I have no issue with you or your people; let us go our separate ways in peace. I am from India, a country of which you have never heard, and I am looking for other members of my country who are in Aadra and from whom I have separated.

He asked, pointing to the north, "You're going there." I answered, "I am.

He remained silent for a while, seemingly deliberating on something. He finally started to speak. What is that, he questioned. What is that, exactly? He pointed at my pistol first, then my rifle.

They are weapons, I said, "weapons that kill from very far away." I indicated the female swimmers in the pool below us. With this, I could kill as many of those women as I wanted without moving from where we are standing, I said, tapping my pistol.

He gave me a puzzled look, but I persisted. And with this," I said, balancing my rifle in the palm of my right hand, "I could take out one of those far-off warriors." I then waved my left hand in the direction of the hunters' tiny silhouettes in the far north.

The man chuckled. He mockedly commanded, "Do it, and maybe I'll believe the rest of your strange story."

But I added, "I don't want to kill any of them."

Why should I?

Why not, he argued. "They were ready to kill you after imprisoning you. Even now, if they got their hands on you, they will kill you and devour your meat. But I also understand why you won't try it; it's because you've told lies about how your weapon won't be lethal at a great distance. It is merely a strangely constructed club. You could be no more than a lowly Shailtaah, for all I know."

Why would you want me to murder your own citizens? I queried.

He replied proudly, "They are no longer my people." Last night, in the dead of the night, I received the call. The thought that I had risen suddenly entered my head in that manner, and he cleverly struck his hands together. I've been looking forward to becoming a Pahadi for a very long time. Today I travel to the "virana" (literally, "no man's land") between the Gorkha and the Pahadi, where I make my bow, arrows, and shield. I also go red deer hunting for the leather jerkin that will serve as the emblem of my new subdivision.

But I questioned, "Why do you want to kill me?"

He appeared perplexed before finally giving up. "I don't know", he acknowledged. "In Aadra, that is how it is. It is wise to kill anyone who is not a member of one's own tribe lest they kill you. I hid in my cave this morning until the others had left to go hunting because I knew they would find out right away that I had turned into a Pahadi and would kill me. If they discover me, they will kill me, and the Pahadi will also if they find me before I have obtained my Pahadi weapons and jerkin.

When you claim that your weapons can kill at a great distance, I know you are lying because you would kill me if you could. If they existed, you would have murdered me long ago. Come! There isn't any more time for me to talk. She is beautiful, so I will spare her and take her to the Pahadi. He then moved toward me while raising his spear.

I had my rifle ready at my hip. He was so close that all I had to do to send him into Swarga whenever I wanted was to pull the trigger. Despite this, I hesitated. It was hard for me to bring myself to kill someone. Although I had no ill will toward this savage barbarian who behaved almost entirely on instinct like a wild animal, I was still determined to find a way to stop what now seemed inevitable. When he suggested taking her with him, Maya stood by my shoulder with her knife ready in her hand and a sneer on her lips.

As soon as I prepared to fire, the women below us began screaming in unison. I observed the man pause and cast a downward glance, so I followed his lead and focused on the panic and what was causing it. The women were ostensibly leaving the pool and making their way slowly back toward the caves when they came face to face with a gigantic cave-lion, which was standing between them and the cliffs in the middle of the congested path that led to the pool. The women were running hysterically back to the pool while screaming.

The man said with a hint of excitement, "It will do them no good. There is one there, he continued, "whom I hoped would soon follow me to the Pahadi, but it will do them no good, for the lion will wait until they come out and take as many he can carry. Together, we have advanced since the beginning. He held his spear poised above his head, ready to thrust it downward at the lion. He murmured, "She is nearest to him. She won't ever come to me among the Pahadi or again in the future because he will get her. It has no use! No warrior currently alive is capable of throwing a weapon such a distance.

Ignoring him, I aimed my rifle at the large brute below, ready to fire and pulled the trigger as soon as he stopped talking. My bullet must have narrowly missed the target because it smashed the brute's spine behind his shoulders and tore through his heart, killing him instantly. The sound of the rifle briefly shocked the women, but once they realised that their enemy had been killed by the loud noise, they cautiously crept back to examine the corpse.

The person I turned toward as soon as I finished shooting, in case he continued his threatened attack, stood there marvelling and admiring me.

“Why didn't you kill me long ago if you could do that,” he inquired.

I retorted, "I told you I have no quarrel with you. I don't like to kill men I don't have a grumble with... "

But he could not seem to process the thought. He acknowledged, "I can now believe that you are not of Aadra, for no Aadraian would have permitted such an opportunity to escape him." The tribes of the west coast and even the Pahadi of the east coast are much less ferocious than he would have me believe, so I later discovered that he had overstated this. "And your weapon, too!" he exclaimed. "I believed your words to be a lie, but you spoke the truth." Then all of a sudden: "Let's become friends!" he said.

I looked at Maya. I questioned, "Can I trust him?"

Yes, she answered. Why not? Has he not requested friendship?

Sincerity and loyalty are two of the strongest traits of Aadraian people, but at the time I was not familiar with them well enough to know this. They lack the cultural sophistication to have mastered deceit, treason, and hypocrisy. Of course, there are a few exemptions.

The warrior added, "We can travel north together. "You can fight for me, and I'll fight for you. I will continue to serve you until my last breath because you saved Jwala, whom I had declared dead." The palms of his two hands were placed over his eyes as he threw down his spear. I asked Maya, who responded as best she could that this was the Aadraian oath of allegiance in written form. After this, you won't need to be afraid of him, she added.

I questioned, "What should I do?"

She said, "Take his hands out from under his eyes and give him his spear back."

I followed her advice, and the man appeared to be very happy. I then enquired as to what I ought to have done if I had decided against accepting his friendship. They told me that if I had left, the warrior and I would have turned into mortal foes once again the moment I was out of his sight. "But he was defenseless and I could have easily killed him!" I shouted.

"Yes," the warrior acknowledged, "but no man with good sense closes his eyes in front of someone he does not trust.

It was a decent compliment that showed me how much I could rely on the loyalty of my new friend. Given that he knew the country and was obviously a fearless warrior, I was happy to have him with us. I wished I could have found a battalion like him to recruit.

Vinasha, the warrior advised that since the women were now nearing the cliffs, we should head to the valley before they could stop us because they might try to detain us and were almost certainly going to attack Maya. We hurriedly descended the rocky path, arriving at the base of the cliffs just ahead of the women. They yelled at us to stop, but we continued to move quickly because we didn't want to cause any trouble, that would have only result in their deaths. After travelling about a mile, we heard someone calling Vinasha by name from behind us.

When we stopped and turned around, we saw a woman running quickly in our direction.

Vinasha exclaimed, "It's Jwala!" "Is she crazy to follow me like this?"

The young woman eventually stopped in front of us, panting. She paid no attention to Maya or myself, but as she gazed on Vinasha with her sparkling eyes, she sobbed: "I've gotten up. I've gotten up."

The only thing the man could utter was "Jwala!"

"Yes," she continued, "the call reached me just before I left for the pool; however, I was unaware that it had reached you. My Vinasha, I can see it in your eyes! Together, we shall continue!" In his arms, she threw herself.

It was a heartbreaking sight and it became clear that these two had been partners for a very long time and that each had believed they were about to be split apart by the specific law of evolution that applies in Aadra and was gradually coming into view in front of my bewildered mind. I'm not entirely sure that I do so even now because I did not fully understand the wondrous process that occurs within the boundaries of Swaraj Dweep's barrier cliffs back then.

Vinasha clarified to Jwala that Maya was my woman and deserved same loyalty as me, the one who had killed the cave-lion and saved her life.

Maya and Jwala at first were like two strange cats on a back fence, but soon they started to accept one another like in an armed truce, and quickly became friends. Jwala was an attractive young woman. She was strong and sinuosely built like a tigress while also being feminine and sweet. She eventually won over Maya and me, and I believe she felt the same way about us. Vinasha was very much a man-if you will call him a savage, he was still a man nonetheless.

The novitiates delayed their approach to the Pahadi country so that they could properly fit themselves in the matter of arms and apparel, but Maya and I continued on our way with them because we found that travelling in company with Vinasha made our journey easier and safer.

We grew close as a result, to the point where we regretted the day they took their places among their new comrades and we were left to continue on our journey alone. Vinasha was very worried that the Pahadi would not welcome Maya and me in a friendly manner and that we would therefore need to stay away from them.

Making friends with them would have been very beneficial to us since their nation bordered the Mahans directly. If they had become friends, Maya's dangers would have been all but over and I would have completed the second half of my arduous journey.

Given everything I had been through, I frequently questioned whether I would have a chance to finish the journey in quest of my friends. The dangers would grow more terrifying as I approached the southern half of the island, which was where the Sood and the Kannanaukas lived and where the more horrifying reptilia had their stamping grounds. And if I did not find the other members of my party by then, what would become of me? No area of Aadra that I was familiar with would allow me to survive for very long; once my ammunition ran out, I should be effectively dead.

There was a chance the Mahans would accept me, but even Maya could not say so with certainty. Even if they did, could I go back to where I had started after failing to locate my own people and travel to the Mahans' far northern land? I had my doubts.

However, Maya, who was more or less a fatalist, taught me a philosophy that was as essential to Aadra's mental tranquilly as faith is to the devoted Hindu of the outside planet.

***

*

Soon after leaving the cliff dwellings of the Gorkha, we were relaxing in front of a small fire in a secure grotto one evening when Jwala posed a question that I had never considered asking Maya. She questioned her about why she had left her own people and how she had travelled to the Sood nation, where I had discovered her.

Maya initially resisted giving an explanation, but eventually agreed, and for the first time I heard the full account of her upbringing and experiences. She provided more explanation for my benefit than would have been required if I were a native Aadraian.

Maya began, "I am a Vishesh," and then she turned to face me. A Vishesh, according to Krishna, is a woman who was created from nothing and did not originate from an egg. Aarambh "My mother was nursing me when I was a baby. These only occur rarely and only among the Mahans. Most of us are caught by the Bhootnath, but my mother kept me hidden until I grew to a size where the Bhootnath could not easily tell me apart from someone who had started from the bottom. I was the only person who could have known my mother and father. High chief among the Mahans is my father. In order for their offspring to be Vishesh, or born as are all the children of your race, my Krishna, as you tell me is the fact, one of them-likely my mother-had to complete the seven cycles, or roughly seven hundred years.

His name is Mahamaya, and he and my mother both came up from the beginning. The men of my people sought me out because I was different from them in that my children like me, would likely be more advanced than they were. However, none of them had any appeal for me and I had nothing in my mind too. The most persistent was Eklavya, a powerful warrior whom my father greatly feared to usurp his position as the chieftain of the Mahans. He had a sizable following among the younger Mahans, the ones that had recently risen from the Pahadi, and since this class is typically numerically much more powerful than the older Mahans, as well as considering that he knows no bounds, we have long anticipated that he would find some justification for a break with Mahamaya the High Chief, my dad.

One of the hunter returned late night and informed my father in a trembling tone how he chanced upon Eklavya talking to a Bhootnath in a lonely place far from the village, and that plainly he had heard the words: "If you will help me, I will help you-I will deliver into your hands all Visheshs among the Mahans.' This added another layer of difficulty. Eklavya wanted me, but I would have none of him.

When my father heard this, he was furious, but he was also afraid for me, "who is Vishesh?" He summoned me, narrated the whole ordeal and suggested two strategies in which we might annoy Eklavya. The first was that if I became what he is, he would be reluctant to give me to the Bhootnath or to continue keeping the wicked agreement he had made, which would doom his own children, who would undoubtedly be as I am, their mother. The other option was to flee until Eklavya was subdued and punished. I made the latter decision and took off southward.

The Bhootnath, who typically only seek the best Mahans, pose little threat outside the borders of the Mahan country. This is for two very good reasons: One is that there has always been rivalry between the Bhootnath and the Mahans over who will rule the world in the long run. Most people seem to agree that the race that becomes the first to evolve to the point where they can produce offspring of both sexes and members of their own species must rule over all other beings.

However, the Bhootnath only produce males, which is why they steal our young females. By stealing Vishesh, they increase their own chances of eventually reproducing both sexes while simultaneously decreasing ours. The Bhootnath first started to produce their own kind-after which evolution from Mahan to Bhootnath ceased gradually, until now it is unknown.

The Mahans already produce both sexes, but because the Bhootnath watch us so closely, very few males live to adulthood, and even fewer females escape abduction. It is a strange situation because even though our greatest enemies despise and fear us, they dare not kill us because they understand that without us, they would also go extinct. "Ah, but we could, if we once get a start, I am sure that when all were true Visheshs there would have been atlast the true dominant race before which all the world would be forced to bow."

Maya always talked about the world as if it ended at Aadra. She didn't seem to understand my origins or that there were a great number of other people outside of her stern barrier-cliffs. She seemed to think that I came from a totally different planet. She refused to bother her pretty head about matters that were completely beyond her, such as where it was and how I arrived in Aadra .

“So I fled to hide,” she continued with the intention of passing the cliffs south of Mahan and finding a refuge in the Pahadi country. There didn't seem to be any other viable option, hence I took the risk.

The following day, I crossed into the Pahadi country and took refuge in a large cave, where I felt that I was reasonably safe from the Bhootnath, though threatened by numerous other dangers. To a Vishesh, any fate is preferable to being captured by the terrifying Bhootnath, from whose land no one ever returns.

"After sleeping soundly for a while, I was startled by a faint noise coming from inside the cavern. I could see the terrifying silhouette of a Bhootnath against the bright moonlight that illuminated the entrance. No way out existed. The cave's entrance was small and narrow. I lay motionless, hoping against hope that the creature had simply stopped here to rest and would soon leave without noticing me, even though I was aware that he had come looking for me.

"I watched as the creature crept silently toward me, its large eyes glowing in the darkness of the cave. At last, I realised that those eyes were fixed on me, as the Bhootnath can see in the dark more clearly than a lion or a tiger. There was only a short distance left between us when I leaped on my feet and sprinted frantically in his direction in an attempt to get past him and escape to the outside of the cave. It was obviously insane because even if I would temporarily succeed, the Bhootnath would have simply followed and swooped down on me from above. As it was, he reached out and grabbed me, and despite my resistance, he was able to overcome me. He was nearly ripped out of his long, white robe during the duel, and in his rage, he trembled and beat his wings together.

He asked me my name, but I refused to say it, which infuriated him even more. He finally dragged me to the cave's entrance, picked me up in his arms, spread his huge wings, and then leaped into the air while flapping all through the night. As the moonlit landscape disappeared beneath me, I noticed that we had already left the water and were travelling to the Bhootnath nation of Haveli.

"A loud whirring of enormous wings could be heard coming from above as the shadowy shapes of Haveli were taking shape beneath us. The Bhootnath and I both looked up at the same time to see two enormous Danavas (flying reptiles called pterodactyls) swooping down on us. The Bhootnath spun and descended almost to sea level before sprinting southward to get away from our pursuer. Despite their enormous size, the large creatures are swift on their wings, but the Bhootnath are faster.

Bhoothnath continued to maintain his lead even with my additional weight, but he was unable to extend it. We sped along the coast in a southernly direction through the night, faster than the fastest wind. The Danavas kept trailing us even when we reached great heights where the air was chilly and the world below was little more than a haze of blurry outlines.

When I finally noticed that the Bhootnath was fainting, I knew we had travelled a great distance because the wind's rush against my face attested to how quickly we had advanced. However, I was unsure of our location at the time. My captor had to turn in toward the coast after one of the Danavas gained on us and was able to head us. He was pushed to the left further and further as they did so, sinking lower and lower. His breathing became more laboured, and the motion of his formerly powerful wings became weaker.

When they passed by, we were at the edge of a forest and not ten feet above the ground. One of them grabbed the Bhootnath by his right wing, and as he struggled to get away, he released his hold on me and knocked me to the ground. I jumped to my feet like an ecca in fear and ran for safety into the forest, where I knew neither could pursue or seize me. Then I turned around and peered behind me to see two enormous reptiles tearing my kidnapper apart and immediately devouring him. "I was saved, but I still felt lost. I had no idea how far away the Mahans nation was from me, and it didn't appear likely that I would ever be able to return there in safety.

The day was just beginning, and the carnivores would soon be stalking out to make their first kill. I had only my knife with me. A strange landscape surrounded me; the flowers, trees, and even the grasses were dissimilar to those in my northern home, and soon a creature fully as repulsive as the Bhootnath-a hairy man thing that could hardly walk upright-appeared before me. I shivered before running away. I escaped the horrifying perils that my ancestors had faced in the early stages of their human evolution, but the hairy monster that had discovered me was relentlessly pursuing me. Others of his kind later joined him. My Krishna, you saved me from the silent men known as the Sood. You have been with me on my adventures since then, and I would go through them all again if it meant meeting you.

She said that in a very kind way, which I greatly appreciated. She seemed like a very nice young lady whose friendship anyone would be happy to have, but I wished that the strange thrills I experienced when she touched me wouldn't happen. It was extremely unsettling and it made me think of love, and I was certain that I could never love this crude little barbarian.

Maya shuddered so violently at even the slightest mention of the name that I was reluctant to press the issue, so the Bhootnath still remained a mystery to me. Until this point, I had thought of the Bhootnath as a purely mythological creature.

Although I was very interested in the Bhootnath, I didn't have much time to reflect on them because we spent most of our waking hours focusing on survival, which is the main activity of Aadraians. As we could not accompany Vinasha and Jwala without putting ourselves in grave danger and running the risk of endangering them, they had to depart from us. However, they both swore to always be our friends and assured us that should we ever need their assistance, we had only to ask; I could not doubt their sincerity given that we had played such an important role in bringing them safely to the Pahadi village.

We had only one more day together. We should split up in the late afternoon, with Vinasha and Jwala going directly to the Pahadi village and Maya and I taking a detour to avoid the archers. When the time came for them to enter the village of their new people, they were both displaying signs of nervous apprehension, but they were also both very proud and happy. They assured us that they would be well received because tribes always welcome new members, especially as distance from the origin grows and the higher tribes or races become numerically much weaker than the lower ones.

The Kannanaukas, or apes, populate the southernmost part of the island in fairly large numbers. The Sood, who are slightly more numerous than the Kannanaukas, are followed by fewer Shailtaah than Sood and fewer Shailatiya than Shailtaah. This continues until there are more Mahans than Pahadi, at which point the law is the opposite because the Mahans outpaces the Pahadi. The reason for this, as Maya explained to me, is that even though evolution essentially stopped with the Mahans and they still remain with them today, there is no less among them on this score. Mahans arrived from both the west and east coasts. Additionally, there are fewer carnivorous reptiles at the northern tip of the island as well as fewer of the large, ferocious cats that kill so many people in the southern races.

I was beginning to understand the Aadraian theory of evolution by this point, which helped to explain why the races I had seen up to this point lacked young. Coming from the beginning, the Aadraian goes through all of the stages of evolution-or at least many of them-that the human race has gone through over the countless ages since life first began to stir on a new planet. However, the question that persisted in my mind was, "What created the world at the beginning, Aarambh?"

I had noticed that the land had gradually risen as we had left the Sood country and moved north, and that we were now several hundred feet above the level of the inland sea. Maya explained to me that the Mahans region was still considerably higher and colder, which explained why there weren't many reptiles there. Even more pronounced than the stages of man's evolution was the change in the shape and types of the lower animals.

In the land of the Pahadi, the diminutive ecca, or small horse, developed into a hardy little pony. The number of small lions and tigers increased, though many of the large ones remained. The woolly mammoth and several varieties of Labyrinthadonta were also more prevalent. These creatures, from which God help me, I should have anticipated finding further south, but for some mysterious reason they bulk up most in the Pahadi and Mahan countries, despite being thankfully uncommon. They seem to be a very primitive life form that is quickly approaching extinction in Aadra, but wherever they are found, they pose a threat to all life.

Midway through the afternoon, Vinasha and Jwala bid us farewell. The village of Pahadi was not far away; in fact, we had come much closer than we had anticipated. Mayaand I were to take a detour in the direction of the sea while our companions went straight in hunt of the Pahadi chief.

When I saw what was ahead of us, I immediately pulled back into cover and pushed Maya behind me. Maya and I had travelled perhaps a mile or two and were about to emerge from a dense wood. I observed a group of Gorkha warriorsbig, intimidating-looking men. I could tell they were marching back toward their caves because of the direction they were going, and if we stayed where we were, they would pass by without noticing us. Just then Maya poked me and said in a hushed tone, "They have a prisoner." “He's a Pahadi,” I said.

He was the first fully grown Pahadi I had come across. He was a tall, straight, handsome savage with a regal bearing. Vinasha was a handsome man, but every aspect of this Pahadi’s appearance showed that he belonged on a higher evolutionary plane. Vinasha was just entering the Pahadi sphere, whereas this man, it seemed to me, must be very close to the next stage of his development and would make him an envied Mahan.

I muttered to Maya, "They'll kill him.

I shivered because I had just narrowly avoided the same fate when she said, "The dance of death." It seemed cruel that someone who must have survived all the terrifying stages of human evolution within Aadra would pass away just below his objective. I carefully targeted a Gorkha and raised my rifle to my shoulder. Since another was right behind the first, if I hit him, I would actually hit two people.

I felt Maya touch my arm. She inquired, "What would you do?" All of them are our enemies.

"Enemy or no enemy," I said, "I'm going to save him from the dance of death," and I pulled the trigger. The two Gorkha jumped forward on their faces in response to the command. I gave Maya my rifle and, after pulling out my pistol, stepped outside in full view of the surprised group. When the rifle's muzzle noise was heard, the Gorkha did not flee like some of the lower classes of Aadraians did. Instead, as soon as they spotted me, they started yelling demonic war cries before charging at me while raising their spears above their heads.

The Pahadi observed the events from a still, lifeless position. Despite the fact that his feet were unbound and no warriors were left to watch him, he made no attempt to flee. Ten of the Gorkha were pursuing me. As quickly as a man could count to three, I dropped three of them with my pistol. Then, as my rifle sounded close to my left shoulder, another one of them stumbled and fell to the ground. Maya is so brave! Although I had taught her how to sight, aim, and squeeze the trigger rather than pull it, she had never fired a shot in her entire life. She had frequently practised these new skills, but I never imagined that they would turn her into a markswoman so rapidly.

Six of their comrades were easily killed, and the remaining six took cover behind some low bushes and were probably planning their next move. I on the other hand was out of ammunition and worried about the next attack. I wished they would leave because they were already quite close to us. One of them suddenly stood up and hurled his spear. It was the most amazing display of speed I've ever seen. I got the impression that he had just started to stand up straight when the weapon was halfway there, hurtling like an arrow in his direction. When that small life was in danger, I took the best shot I have ever taken in my life. I didn't intentionally aim; instead, it seemed as though my subconscious mind was driving me rather than self-preservation. Maya was in peril. A streak of incandescent powder marked the path of the bullet from its muzzle just as my pistol was flying into position, and the spear, with its point broken, was deflected from its path. The six Gorkha emerged from their shelter with a howl of dismay and fled towards south.

I swivelled to face Maya. Her eyes were wide and she was very pale because she was almost in the death's grasp. Despite this, she forced a small smile and an expression of great pride into her eyes. She yelled, "My Krishna!" and took hold of my hand. "My Krishna!" and a hand pressure were all that was said. My Krishna! My chest started to feel stirred. Was it astonishment or consternation? Impossible! I abruptly turned away from her.

"Come!" I continued, then marched over to the Pahadi prisoner.

The Pahadi stood there with stoic indifference as he observed us. He probably anticipated being killed, but he didn't exhibit any outward signs of fear if he did. His keenest focus was on either my pistol or the rifle that Maya was still carrying, which showed how much he was interested in them. My knife was used to cut his bonds. As I was doing this, a look of surprise tinged and animated his haughty reserve. He gave me a puzzled look.

He questioned, "What are you going to do with me?"

I responded, "You are liberated. "If you'd like, go home."

He asked, "Why don't you kill me?" "I have no defence,"

"Why should I kill you? To save your life, I put my life and the life of this young woman in danger. Why then should I take it right now?" Naturally, I didn't say "young lady" because there isn't a Aadraian term for that; however, I have to give myself a lot of leeway when translating Aadraian conversations. It may be literal to refer to a lovely young girl as "she," but it doesn't seem very valorous.

The Pahadi fixed his level, unwavering gaze on me for at least a minute. Then he continued to talk.

He questioned, "Man of strange skins, who are you? "You are not Mahan, Pahadi, Gorkha, or any other type of man I have seen before, but your wife is Mahan. Tell me where such a strong warrior and a kind adversary come from."

"It is a long story, but let me just say that I am not Aadra-born," I replied. Let that sink in: I am a stranger here and I am not your enemy. With the exception of the Mahan warrior Eklavya, I have no desire to be anyone's enemy in Aadra."

Eklavya, he cried out. "You oppose Eklavya, don't you? Then why?" I responded, "Because he would hurt Maya." You've heard of him?

He can't know him, Maya said. "As everyone does when they enter a new sphere, Eklavya emerged from the Pahadi long ago and adopted a new name. Since there is no sexual activity between the Pahadi and the Mahan, he cannot know him."

The fighter grinned. "Eklavya, who had relations with the Pahadi, had risen not long ago-so recently, in fact, that he was difficult for him to recall-and recently decided to disregard the long-standing laws of Aadra. Eklavya, who would be the Mahans tribe's chief, has asked the Pahadi for assistance."

Maya was horrified. The piece was amazing. Pahadi and Mahan had never been close friends because of the brutal laws of Aadra, which are the only way the various races can continue to be distinct from one another.

Maya questioned, "Will the Pahadi join him?" Will they invade Mahamaya my father's country?

The younger Pahadi support the plan because they think they will instantly turn into Mahans, the warrior retorted. They want to transform into Mahans in a single step by crossing the many years of change that they will experience naturally. They will not be Mahans until the time comes when they are ready to rise, we of the older

Pahadi tell them, even though they live in Mahan territory and wear their skins and ornaments. We also inform them that even then, some of them will never rise, and that they will never truly become a Mahan race.

As our people occasionally raid the Mahan country for booty, it is acceptable; however, trying to conquer and hold it would be insane. I, for one, was content to wait until I received the call. I believe that it won't be long now.

What's your name, Maya enquired. The man replied, "Bheeshma."

"You are the Pahadi chief?" Maya went on.

Bheeshma responded, "No, Shoor is the leader of the Pahadi of the east. And he opposes the idea of invading the nation of my father?

Unfortunately, given that he has recently come to believe that he is vardhanah, he is actually quite in favour of it, the man said. He has been serving as a Pahadi chief since I moved there from Gorkha and I have not noticed any changes in him . He still gives off the impression of being more Gorkha than Pahadi.

Shhoor would never agree to hold a subordinate position, and once he plants a victorious foot in Mahan, he will not move away from the fight. However, he is a good chief and a mighty warrior, and if Eklavya convinces him to his cause, the Mahans may find themselves under a Pahadi chieftain soon.

Since I had never heard the word "vardhanah" before, I enquired as to what it meant. When used to describe a person's evolutionary progress in Aadra, it literally translates as through, finished, or done-for. With this knowledge, the intriguing fact that not every person can progress through every stage to that of Mahan was developed. Some people never advance past the Markat stage, while others become Shailtaah, Shailatiya, Gorkha, or Pahadi. First generation Kannanaukas have the potential to become Sood, second generation Sood have the potential to become Shailtaah, third generation Shailtaah need to become Gorkha, and so on until the parent of a sixth generation Pahadi.

Even with this explanation, it was still not entirely clear to me because I didn't understand how different generations of peoples could exist who supposedly had no progeny. However, I started to see a faint outline of the laws that control reproduction and evolution in this peculiar land. Since neither pleasure nor cleanliness could be obtained from what appeared to be a religious ritual, I already knew that the warm pools that always surround every tribal residence were closely connected with the Aadraian scheme of evolution. I also knew that the daily immersion of the females in the greenish, slimy water was a response to some natural law.

However, I remained lost, and it didn't seem that Maya could enlighten me because she was forced to use words that I did not understand and whose meanings she was unable to clarify.

A hundred Pahadi warriors suddenly materialised in a rough circle around us as we were standing there talking, startling us. There was a commotion in the nearby bushes and tree limbs. They came slowly, their heavy bows loaded with long, sharp arrows, and they greeted Bheeshma with a barrage of inquiries. They initially regarded Maya and me with hostility and suspicion, but after hearing Bheeshma, their demeanour changed to one of friendliness. All the talking was done by a huge savage. He had the build of a mountain but was proportionately ideal.

Bheeshma introduced us to Shhoor. Shhoor then questioned me extensively about the country I was from after I had briefly shared my story with him. The other warriors too gathered close to hear my responses, and there were many looks of bewilderment on their faces as I described a different world to them, the yacht that had taken me over vast waters, and the plane that had carried me danava-like over the top of the barrier cliffs. The first outspoken scepticism about me came after I mentioned the hydroaeroplane, and Maya had to defend me.

She exclaimed, "I saw it with my own eyes!" "I observed him fighting a Danava while he was flying through the air. When the Sood realised I was being pursued, they fled."

Shhoor abruptly exclaimed, "Whose is she?" with his eyes locked adamantly on Maya.

There was silence for a split second. Maya raised her head and gave me a hurt and perplexed look. Who is she , asked Shhoor again. I responded, "She is mine," even though I was unable to identify the force that had driven me to say it. However, an instant later, I was glad that I had said the words because Maya's proud and joyful expression was a very rewarding incentive.

Shhoor stared at her for a while before turning to face me. He asked, with just a hint of a sneer on his face, "Can you keep her?

My palm was on the grip of the pistol as I replied that I could. When he noticed the movement, he smiled and cast a quick glance at the automatic's butt, which was sticking out of its holster. He turned and raised his large bow, fitted an arrow, and far-removed the shaft. With arrogant grins on their faces, his warriors stood motionless and looked at him. The longest and heaviest bows of them all were his. One would need to be incredibly strong to bend it, but Shhoor effortlessly pulled the shaft back until the stone point touched his left forefinger.

He then brought up the shaft to the level of his right eye, held it there for a split second, and then let it go. Half of the arrow's length was sticking out of a six inch tree fifty feet away when the arrow came to a stop. With expressions of great satisfaction on their faces, Shhoor and his warriors turned to face me. Then, seemingly for Maya's benefit, the chieftain strutted back and forth a few times, swinging his massive arms and broad shoulders like a wasted prize fighter at a dancing area at a beach.

I realised a response was required, so I quickly drew my gun, dropped it on the still-quivering arrow, and then pulled the trigger. The Pahadi jumped backwards and raised their weapons at the sound of the command, but as I grinned, they gained courage and lowered them again, following my gaze to the tree. The shaft of their chief was gone, and through the trunk was a tiny round hole that indicated the trajectory of my bullet.

If I do say so myself, it was a good shot, determination and necessity must have guided that bullet; I just had to make a good shot so I could right away claim my place among those barbaric and war like Aadraians of the sixth sphere. Although its impact was immediately apparent, I'm not sure if it aided my cause with Shhoor. While he might have been content to tolerate me as a fun and interesting curiosity, he now seemed to be thinking negatively about me based on the change in his expression.

Knowing this type, I can't help but wonder if I didn't make him look foolish in the eyes of his warriors by defeating him at his own game. Whose king-civilized or savage-could tolerate such impudence? When I noticed his grimaces, I decided it would be best to end the chanced encounter and go on our way, especially for Maya's sake. However, just as I was about to do that, Shhoor stopped us with a gesture and his warriors surrounded us. "What does this mean?" you ask. Bheeshma spoke up on our behalf before Shhoor could respond to my demand.

Shhoor questioned, "Is this the expression of a Pahadi chieftain's gratitude to one who has served you by rescuing one of your soldiers from the enemy-rescuing him from the Gorkha dance of death?"

After a brief period of silence, Shhoor cleared his brow and while struggling to maintain a semblance of a smile, spoke : "No harm will come to the stranger. I only wanted to keep him so he could be fed tonight in Shhoor's village. He is free to go his way in the morning. Shhoor won't stand in his way."

Although I wasn't completely at ease, I still wanted to explore the interior of the Pahadi village and knew that if Shhoor wanted to betray me, I wouldn't be any more in his control in the morning than I was at the moment. In fact, during the night, I might find a way to flee with Maya, whereas at the moment neither of us could hope to escape the circling warriors unscathed. I promptly and politely accepted his invitation, in order to allay any fears I might have had about his sincerity.

His happiness was apparent, and as we walked toward his village, he walked beside me and frequently enquired about my world, its people, and their custom. He appeared to be very perplexed by the idea that we could travel anywhere day or night without the worry of being eaten by ferocious animals or savage reptiles, and when I told him about the vast armies that we kept, his simple mind could not comprehend the idea that they were only there to kill people.

"I'm glad I don't live in your country among such barbarous peoples, he said. In Aadra, men of different races fight one another when they come into contact, but their weapons are primarily used to kill beasts during pursuit and defence.

Unlike your people, we don't make weapons solely for killing people. You are fortunate to have escaped to Aadra's peace and security from your apparently barbaric home country."

After what I had told Shhoor about the great war that had been raging in Europe for more than two years before I left home, I couldn't object to this fresh perspective either. Three terrifying creatures attacked us while we were on the march to the Pahadi village, but Shhoor handled it all like it was nothing out of the ordinary, charging forward with his spear raised or driving a heavy shaft into the attacker's body before continuing our conversation.

Two of his band members were mauled, and one was killed by a large, ferocious rhinoceros, but he did not fret about it neither did they mourned the dead. The corpse were stripped of their possessions and left in the place where they had passed away; the carnivora would take care of his interment. An Indian big-game hunter would have been green with envy at the trophies that these Pahadi left for the meat eaters. However, they were already fairly heavily burdened with the spoils of the hunt, and their decision to do so was only motivated by their particular fondness for rhino meat. They did, after all, cut all the edible parts from the rhino and carried them home.

Those who left the hide on the items they chose because they want tough hide for various uses, including sandals, shield covers, knife hilts, and other items. My interest in their shields increased after I witnessed one being used to fend off a saber-toothed tiger attack. The large animal suddenly charged us as it lay up after eating in a cluster of dense bushes. Barrages of spears were hurled at it, some of which completely pierced its body due to their force.

Due to the charge's close proximity, spears were used instead of bows and arrows. However, after the spears were launched, the men who were not in the charge's direct path quickly fired bolt after bolt into the large carcass. I stood helpless with my rifle out of fear of shooting one of the warriors closing in on it as the beast, screaming in pain and rage, bore down on Bheeshma.

Bheeshma was prepared, though. He set aside his bow and knelt in front of his large oval shield, which had a six-inch-diameter hole in the middle. He had a heavy knife in his right hand and a shield that was tightly looped around his left arm. Bheeshma was completely covered by the shield as the large cat, bristling with spears and arrows, threw itself upon it. Bheeshma then fell on his back. While Bheeshma repeatedly stabbed the ferocious animal in the vitals through the round hole in the shield's centre, the tiger clawed and bit at the thick rhinoceros hide with which the shield was faced. Even if I had not intervened, the battle probably would have gone to Bheeshma;

however, when I saw a clear opening and no Pahadi beyond, I raised my rifle and dispatched the beast.

Bheeshma got up and looked at the sky, saying it looked like rain. The others had already started marching again toward the village. The matter was resolved. The entire situation reminded me, for no apparent reason, of a friend who once shot a cat in his backyard. He did not speak of anything else for three weeks.

When we arrived at the village, a sizable palisaded enclosure with several hundred leaf-thatched huts arranged in groups of two to seven, it was almost dark. When grouped, the hexagonal huts were joined together to resemble the cells of a bee hive. Each additional hut in a group denoted an additional female, with one hut signifying a warrior and his mate.

Strong creepers were planted at the base of the logs and trained to weave in and out to bind them together to form a solid wall, which served as the palisade that encircled the village. The longer pieces were supported a little bit above their centres of equilibrium by shorter logs that were embedded in the ground at right angles to the longer ones. The longer pieces were tilted outward at an angle of about thirty degrees. Sharpened stakes had been driven at various angles along the top of the palisade.

The only entrance to the enclosure was through a narrow opening that was three feet wide and three feet high. This opening was sealed from the inside by two braced logs that paralleled the inside face of the wall and two logs that were about six feet long and laid horizontally, one on top of the other, between the inside face of the palisade.

Bheeshma graciously explained the service we had provided him to the curious warriors and women who greeted us as we entered the village. After hearing this, they showered us with their well-intentioned attentions, as it seemed Bheeshma was a very well-liked tribesman. They loaded us down with necklaces made of lion and tiger teeth, pieces of dried meat, exquisitely tanned hides, and exquisitely decorated earthen pots, all the while Shhoorglared angrily at us, seemingly resentful of the attention paid to us because we had served Bheeshma.

We eventually arrived at a hut that they had set aside for us, where we cooked our meat and some vegetables the women had brought. We also ate cheese made from the milk of wild goats and milk from cows, as well as honey, thin bread made from wheat flour that they had ground themselves, grapes, and fermented grape juice. This was the first milk I had ever had in Aadra. It was quite possibly the most delicious meal I had since leaving the Jalayana and its colourful chef, Vishvesh J. Sudarshana, who could make chicken taste like heaven and pork chops taste like chicken.

***

*

After meal, with Maya's head pillowed in my lap and a sense of immense contentment permeating me, I rolled a cigaret and stretched out at ease before the doorway on a pile of furs. I hadn't experienced any sense of tranquilly or security since my plane had topped Aadra's barrier cliffs. My hand strayed to the girl I had claimed as mine, to her luscious hair, and to the golden fillet that held it close to her attractive head. I gathered her in my arms and crushed her to me, smothering her mouth with a long, long kiss as her slender fingers groping upward sought mine and drew them to her lips.

But now, men could be heard hollering from beyond the palisade, toward the main gate, and the guard was responding to calls and questions. We did hear. Undoubtedly returning hunters. In the midst of the howling dogs, we heard them enter the village. I neglected to mention the Pahadi dogs. When the herd grazed outside of the palisade during the day, they were guarded by gaunt, wolf-like creatures that swarmed the village, ten dogs to every cow. The dogs, with the exception of a few, were brought into the village; these few well-trained brutes remained with the herd. During the night, the cows were herded in an outer enclosure that was roofed against the attacks of the carnivorous cats. They consumed most of the predatory animals that were killed while protecting the herd during the day, so their meager hold was completely worthless.

Maya and I rose to enter the hut shortly after the commotion at the gate had died down, and at the same moment, a warrior emerged from one of the winding alleys that made up the streets of the Pahadi village and run between the haphazardly positioned huts and groups of huts. The man stopped in front of us and spoke to me, telling me that Shhoor wanted me to visit his hut. The invitation's wording and the messenger's demeanour completely caught me off guard; they were both friendly and respectful, and as a result, I went voluntarily, telling Maya that I would be back soon.

When we took over the hut, I put my weapons and ammo aside, and I now left them with Maya because I had noticed that the men of Pahadi did not carry weapons outside of their hunting knives in the village streets. After what I had gone through in Aadra, I had not anticipated the atmosphere of peace and security that pervaded this village, and I believe it must have numbed my faculties of judgement and reason. I had consumed the lotus flower of safety; threats were no longer present because they had vanished.

The messenger guided me through the maze-like lanes to a large open space close to the village's centre. The longest hut I had yet seen was located at one end of this plaza, and there were numerous warriors standing in front of its door. I could make out that the interior was lit and that many men had gathered there. The dogs in the plaza were thick as fleas, and the ones I got close to showed a strong desire to devour me. They did not pay any attention to my companion but seemed to realize I was an alien. When I finally entered the council-hut for that is what it appeared to be, I discovered a sizable concourse of warriors seated-or rather, squatting-all over the floor.

Shhoor and another warrior who I immediately recognised as a Mahan stood at one end of the oval space the warriors left down the middle of the room, and then I noticed that there were many Mahans present. There were several flaming torches positioned around the walls and inserted into holes in the clay plaster, which evidently served to keep the flames from igniting the inflammable wood and grasses that made walls of the hut. There were several ferocious dogs lying around among the warriors or pacing restlessly back and forth.

I was led into the centre of the group towards Shhoor, The Mahans, gave me curious looks as I entered. As I moved forward, I sensed one of the dogs sniffing at my heels. Suddenly, a large brute leaped onto my back. I saw a large Airedale jumping frantically around me as I turned to push it away before its fangs grabbed hold of me. The smiling jaws, half-closed eyes, and back-laid ears communicated to me louder than the words of man that this was not a savage enemy but a joyful friend. When I finally recognised him, I knelt down and wrapped my arms around his neck as he cried out in delight and whined. It was the venerable Dhani. The Dhani of Vishvesh Sudarshana, who had loved me just as much as his boss.

"Where is this dog's owner?" Turning to face Shhoor, I questioned.

The chief cocked his head in the direction of the Mahan who was standing by his side. He responded, "He belongs to Eklavya the Mahan.

I retaliated by saying, "He belongs to Vishvesh J. Sudarshana, Jr., of Banaras, and I want to know where his master is.

Mahan shook his head. He declared, "I own the dog." "He came to me cor-sva-jo and is unlike any other dog in Aadra in that he is both kind and docile and, when roused, a killer. I wouldn't give him up. I am not familiar with the man you mention."

Eklavya saw this, then! Maya had run away from this person. I questioned whether he knew she was in the area. My mind was at ease when they started questioning me because they did not bring up Maya, which made me wonder if they had sent for me because of her. They appeared particularly interested in the strange world from which I had come, my travels to Aadra, and my plans for the future. Since I had nothing to hide, I answered them directly and assured them that all I wanted was to reconnect with my friends and go home. They were a group of tall, slender, and handsome men who were very intimidating.

The leopard-tails of the Mahans protruded from their left shoulders, and around their heads were bands of gold similar to those that Maya wore. Each carried a light blanket with a barbaric yet beautiful design in addition to the deer-skin tunic that made up the majority of their clothing. This was the first weaved cloth I had ever seen in Aadra. Maya didn't have a blanket because she misplaced it while escaping Eklavya's advances. Shhoor indicated that I could go back to my hut after the audience had probably gone on for at least an hour. Dhani had been sleeping peacefully at my feet the entire time, but as soon as I turned to go, he got up and chased after me. Eklavya called to the terrier, but he never even gave him a cursory glance. When Shhoor got up and called after me, I was almost at the doorway leading from the council-hall. He yelled, "Stop!" "Stranger, halt! You are being followed by the Mahan Eklavya's beast."

I responded, "The dog is not Eklavya's." He belong to my friend and seemingly prefers to stay with me until his master is found. I then returned and continued on my path. I had only taken a few steps when I heard noises behind me. At the same time, a man leaned in close and whispered "Saavdhaan!" close to my ear, which is Aadraian for "beware." Vinasha was there. As he finished speaking, he quickly turned away, as if he didn't want anyone to know that he knew who I was. At that same moment, I spun around to see Eklavya following me quickly. Shhoor pursued him, and it was clear that they were both incensed.

Eklavya came menacingly close with a gun half drawn. He repeated, "The beast is mine. Do you intend to steal him?"

"He is neither yours nor mine, and I'm not stealing him," I retorted "I won't stop him from following you if he wants to, but you can't stop him from following me either." I looked at Shhoor. I questioned, "Is that not fair?" 'Let the dog decide who his master is.'

Without waiting for the response Eklavya seized Dhani by the scruff of the neck. I stayed out of it because I anticipated what would happen, and it did. Dhani turned like lightning toward the Mahan, jerked free from his grip, and jumped for his throat with a ferocious growl. The man took a step back, deflected the initial blow with a forceful fist, and then drew his knife to meet the retaliation of Airedale. And if I hadn't talked to Dhani, he would have definitely come back. I yelled at him to stop in a low voice. He hesitated for a brief moment, trembling and baring his teeth as he glared at his adversary, but he was well trained and had been out with me just as much as he had with Vishvesh; in fact, I had the most influence on his early training. He then walked slowly and with very stiff legs to stand beside me.

Red-faced Eklavya would have attacked the two of us if Shhoor hadn't pulled him aside and whispered in his ear. The Mahan then grunted and walked straight back to the other end of the hall, leaving Dhani and I to continue our journey to the hut and Maya. After greeting him warmly and pausing to speak to him. Bheeshma brushed past me without giving any indication that he recognised me as we exited the village square. We were so close that I could have reached out and touched him.

I was perplexed by his actions until I remembered that, despite having forewarned me, Vinasha had not seemed to want to come across as friendly to me. I was trying to come up with an explanation because I couldn't understand their attitude when I heard the sound of a gun and my thoughts were abruptly diverted. I immediately started running, my mind racing with dread because the only guns I had left in the Pahadi country were those I had left inside the cottage with Maya.

She was in risk, I knew this because she was now fairly skilled in handling both the pistol and the rifle, which eliminated the possibility of accidental firing. I couldn't help but be afraid. When I left the hut, I felt that she and I were safe among friends and had no concern for our safety. However, the meeting with Shhoor, Eklavya's presence and bearing, as well as Vinasha and Bheeshma's behaviour, had raised my suspicions. As a result, I now ran along the winding, crowded streets of the Pahadi village with my heart reasonably in my mouth.

As a result of my excellent sense of direction, which has been greatly enhanced over the years I have spent in the mountains, on the plains, and in the deserts of my home state, I was able to return to the hut where I had left Maya with little to no trouble. I yelled her name as I stepped through the doorway. There was silence. Maya was not inside the hut when I struck a light, and my weapons and ammunition had been taken. However, even in the brief time that the flare lasted, I noticed that this had happened before a half-dozen bulky warriors pounced upon me from as many directions.

A growl of rage erupted from the six men as they threw themselves at me. Dhani had slipped my mind. He emerged among those Pahadi fighting men like a demon of hatred, tearing, rending, and ripping with his long teeth and his powerful jaws. They had me on the ground in a matter of seconds, and it goes without saying that the six of them could have kept me there if it weren't for Dhani. As I was struggling to get rid of them, Dhani was springing on them one after another until they were so occupied trying to protect their lives and hides from him that they could only give me a small portion of their attention. Narrator of them was diligently trying to hit me in the head with his stone hatchet, but I caught his arm and simultaneously turned over onto my belly, so it only took a split second for me to get my feet under me and stand up quickly.

I did so while maintaining control of the man's arm and slinging it over one shoulder. I suddenly leaned forward and launched my adversary over my head, causing him to tumble quickly to the other side of the hut. In the dim interior light, I could see that Dhani had already taken care of one of the others, who was lying very still on the ground, while the other four were attacking him with knives and hatchets while still standing.

I quickly moved into the middle of the clash after rushing to one side of the man I had just disarmed and grabbing his hatchet and knife. Without Dhani, who was the only one who could defeat the four of these savage warriors, I would have soon succumbed to ignominious defeat and death. I've never seen anything as agile on its feet or attack with such horrifying ferocity as that enormous Airedale did. Both of these factors played a role in the defeat of our enemies, who, despite being used to the ferocity of terrifying creatures, appeared in shock at the sight of this strange animal from another world engaged in combat alongside his equally strange master. However, they weren't cowards, and Dhani and I were able to finally defeat them only through cooperation. At the same time that Dhani jumped for a man, I would attack his head with the stone hatchet from the opposite side as we both rushed for him.

I heard many feet running toward us from the plaza as the last man fell to the ground. I couldn't try to leave the village without first finding Maya's whereabouts and freeing her if she was being held captive because to be captured right now would mean death. I wasn't at all confident that I could leave the village, but I was certain of one thing: staying put and being captured would be detrimental to both Maya and myself. With Dhani, who was bloody but content, at my heels, I turned down the first alley and slithered away toward the northern part of the village.

I've rarely felt more helpless than I did in that situation, alone and hunted through the maze-like labyrinths of this barbaric society. However, my concern for Maya's safety far outweighed any fear I might have felt for myself. What misfortune awaited her? Who was in charge and where was she? I had my doubts about whether I would live to discover the answers to these questions, but I knew I would gladly risk my life to make the effort. Then why? With all my worry for the safety of my friends who had travelled with me to Swaraj Dweep, especially Vishvesh J. Sudarshana Jr., my best friend of all, I had never before felt the almost paralysing fear for the safety of any other creature, which now alternately sent me into a fever of despair and a cold sweat of anxiety as my mind focused on the fate of half-savage femininity of whose very existence I had not even dreamed of a few short weeks.

What exactly was her hold on me? Was I possessed to the point where my mind refused to function normally and judgement and reason were usurped by an irrational emotion that I adamantly refused to accept as love? I'd never experienced true love. I wasn't in love right now; the idea itself was absurd. What more could I do? Krishna Bisht, the best choice of the late Vishvesh J. Sudarshana, Sr., one among India's leading captains of industry and the greatest person in India. Be in a-a-a-adore with the phrase stuck in my throat when by my own Indian standards, Could Maya be anything else? At home, little Maya, for all her elegance and delicately pigmented skin, would have been classified as a Wangmo by her clothing, by the habits and customs.

Krishna Bisht is in love with Wangmo! The idea made me shiver.

I could have kicked myself for being the snob and the cad that my thoughts had proven me to be-Me!, who had always prided myself on being neither the one nor the other! Then, in a sudden, brilliant flash, the image of Maya as I had last seen her appeared on the screen of recollection, and I lived again the delectable moment in which we had clung to one another, lips on lips, entangled in see-through cloths, as I left her to visit the committee hall of Shhoor.

These thoughts crossed my mind as Dhani and I made our way through the pitch-black village, still hearing the footsteps and voices of those who were looking for us. I couldn't escape the undeniable fact that the small figure my memories and my hopes entwined themselves around was that of Maya-beloved barbarian-along with many other things. A hoarse whisper came from the dark interior of a hut. A man came out next to me as my name was called in a low voice, and I stopped with my knife raised. 'It was Bheeshma'.

Faster, he exclaimed. "In here! This is my property, they won't search it."

I paused and thought back to his earlier behaviour. As if reading my mind, he spoke quickly and said, "I could not communicate with you in the plaza without risking suspicions that could have prevented me from aiding you now. Rumour is that Shhoor has turned against you and would decimate you, this was after Eklavya the Mahan showed up."

Dhani and I followed him into the hut and made our way through a number of chambers before arriving at a remote apartment without windows, where a small lamp sputtered in an unwinnable struggle against the pitch-black darkness. The smoke from burning oil was able to escape through a hole in the roof, but the area was dimly lit. Bheeshma motioned for me to take a seat on a furry hide that was spread out on the earthen floor.

He said, "I'm your friend and I am not as ungrateful as the vardhanah Shhoor. You saved my life from Shhoor and rebel Mahan, Eklavya. I will serve you, and there are others present who will do the same."

“But Maya, where is she?” I asked because I didn't give much thought to my own safety while she was in threat.

He responded, "Maya is safe." We discovered Shhoor and Eklavya’s designs. When the later learned of Maya’s presence, he demanded to bring her; Shhoor agreed that he should have her; however, Vinasha accompanied the warriors who went to get her. Maya pulled the gun in an effort to defend herself, and killed one of the warriors. The weapons were snatched by others during the scruffle and Vinasha took her in his arms.

Vinasha was supposed to take Maya to Shhoor while others took care of the injured man, who was actually already dead. However, instead of taking Maya to Shhoor, Vinasha took her to his own hut, where she is now. Everything happened in a flash. Eklavya tried to take the dog from you while Vinasha and I were in the council-hut. For this, I was looking for Vinasha. He left the council hut right away and went with the warriors to your hut, leaving me behind to observe what was happening there and be of assistance to you if you required it. You are aware of what has occurred since."

I wanted to thank him for his help and asked him to take me to Maya, but he refused because there was a search party in the village. In fact, we could hear them moving back and forth among the cottages and asking questions, so Bheeshma ultimately decided it would be best to go to the vestibule of his dwelling which was actually a number of huts joined together-in order to avoid them entering and searching.

Bheeshma was gone for an extended period of time a few hours that seemed like a forever to me. The commotion outside of my pursuer had long since stopped and I could hear Bheeshma come back from another section of his hut house. I had been worried about him being gone for so long. He seemed agitated and had expression of worry on his face.

What is the issue? I queried. Have they discovered Maya?

"No, I'm afraid Maya has left," he retorted. She escaped when she heard that you had gotten away from them and fled the village. She could not be held by anyone. Armed only with her knife, she made her way outside over the top of the perimeter fence."

“Then I must leave,” I said, standing up. Dhani stood up and shook. When I spoke, he was sound asleep.

Bheeshma concurred, "You must leave right away. Dawn is almost here. At dawn, Eklavya departs to look for her. There are many who will follow and support you," he whispered as he leaned in close to my ear. Shhoorhas agreed to help Eklavya fight the Mahans of Mahamaya, but many of us have banded together to revolt against Shhoor and stop this brutal defacement of the Pahadi and Aadra customs and laws.

We will only rise in the manner that Varuna has commanded. While Bheeshma is alive and is capable of using a powerful blow and a pointy spear with a true Pahadis at his back, no vardhanah may gain access to a Mahan's estate through treachery and force of arms.

I retorted, "I hope that I may live to help you." "I could accomplish a lot more if I had my gears and my ammunition. Do you know where they are ?" "No," he replied, "they have vanished." After that: "Wait! You cannot venture out while only partially armed and dressed in this manner. You must enter the Mahan nation dressed in Mahan clothing. Come!" Without waiting for a response, he led me into a new apartment-or, to be more precise, into one of the many huts that made up his cellular home.

Here was a collection of jewels, weapons, and skins. Bheeshma said, "Remove your odd clothing so that I can dress you as a true Mahan. Here are the trappings of some of them that I killed in my early raids as a Pahadi."

I recognised the wisdom of his advice, and since my clothes were by this point so worn-out that they could only partially hide my nakedness, I had no remorse about putting them aside. After being stripped down to my skin, I put on the red deerskin tunic, leopard tail, golden fillet, armlets, and the leg ornaments of a Mahan, along with the rope, sheath, knife, safeguard, spear, bow, and spear, as well as the long rope, which I learned was the Mahan warrior's hidden blade.

It is a braided rope, much like the ones I remember from my childhood's cow camps at Western plains. The honda is a weight that can be thrown with precision because it is shaped like a golden oval. Bheeshma explained that this large honda is used as a weapon and is cast at an adversary with great force and accuracy before being coiled for a subsequent cast. They employ the noose and the honda in both combat and hunting. A single warrior facing a lone antagonist will attempt to brain his opponent with the metal oval. However, when surrounded by several troops the charger can rope it with noose from various angles.

Since I have been skilled with the rope since I was a young child, I could not have been happier with any other weapon he would have found for me, short of a rifle; however, I must admit that I was less enamoured with my clothing. Given how short and light the tunic was, I might as well have been completely naked from the sensation standpoint. I asked Bheeshma what the Aadraian word for rope was, and he replied, "mah," and for the first time I realised where the word Mahan, which means great ropeman, came from.

I wouldn't have recognised myself if I had been fully equipped due to how odd my clothing and weapons were. My bow, arrows, shield, and short spear were slung across my back; my knife hung from the centre of my girdle; my stone hatchet was affixed to my right hip; and at my left hung the coils of my long rope. I could grab the trident or arrows by having reached my right hand over my left shoulder; my left hand could reach my bow over my right shoulder; and I only needed to perform a veritable super freak move to place my defence in front of me and on my left arm. The tight armlets of gold on the left forearm were primarily relied upon to fend off knife, spear, axe, or arrow attacks from the front; however, when faced with attacks from several adversaries or a big carnivora, using the shield would be more advantageous carried by loops on the left arm.

I followed Bheeshma from his house into the dark, derelict alleys of Pahadi fully equipped, aside from a blanket. We moved silently towards the section closest to the palisade, Dhani silent at our heels. At this point, Bheeshma bid me farewell and expressed his hope to run into me among the Mahans in the near future because he believed "the call would soon come" to him. I expressed my gratitude to him for his steadfast support and made a promise to be there for him in the revolution against Shhoor, regardless of whether I made it to the Mahan nation.

***

*

It took only a moment to run up the palisade's incline and then to fall to the ground outside, or it would have if it weren't for Dhani. After we reached the top, I had to tie my rope around him, lift him over the jagged stakes, and lower him to the ground. Finding Maya in the unknown northern country seemed rather hopeless, but I had to at least try while hoping she would make it through safely and to her dad.

I was astounded by the decreasing populations of ferocious beasts the further north I travelled as Dhani and I swung along in the advancing light of the approaching day. The number of herbivores increased as the number of carnivores decreased, but anywhere in Aadra they were still abundant enough to provide enough food for the meat eaters of each locality. The wild horses, cattle, antelope, and deer I saw had evolved differently from their relatives further south. The horses were bigger, and the kine were less shaggy. A small group of the latter, roughly the size of those on our old Western plains, which the Indians bred in earlier times and to a minor extent even to this day, I saw north of the Pahadi village. They were svelte and fat, and I coveted them with thoughts that any old cow puncher might well surmise I might harbour after having been on the move for weeks. However, they were wary, hardly allowing me to reach within bow-and-arrow range, much less within hooking distance; despite this, I still harboured hopes that I never gave up.

We were chased and charged by man-eaters multiple times before noon, but despite the fact that I was without weapons, Dhani provided me with more than enough protection. Dhani had obviously learned some of the Aadraian hunt customs under the guidance of Eklavya or another Mahan, and of course, he had gained much more knowledge through experience. He was constantly on the lookout for potential threats. He would frequently growl in warning of a large carnivorous animal approaching before I could see it or hear it. When the animal finally showed up, he would run after it snapping at its heels until I could find safety in a tree. Despite this, the cunning Dhani never took an unnecessary risk of being mauled. Even the great cats' lightning fast movements couldn't keep up with him as he would dart in and out with such rapidity. I've witnessed him tease them like this until they legitimately screeched in fury.

The hunters' delay was the biggest interruption to me because they have a nasty tendency to keep one in a tree for an hour or more if they are unsuccessful in their plans. However, when we finally came across a line of cliffs that ran east and west across our path as far as the eye could see in either direction, I knew that we had arrived at the natural border between the Pahadi and Mahan countries. These cliffs' southern face, which rose to a height of about 200 feet and was sheer and precipitous without a break that the eye could see, loomed high and menacing. I had no idea how I was going to find a crossing. I was confused as to whether I should look east toward the even loftier barrier-cliffs fronting the ocean or west toward the inland sea. Was there more than one pass or none? I had no way to find out. I could, but I'll leave it to chance.

The possibility that Dhani had travelled across at least once, if not more than once, and could have guided me to the pass never occurred to me, so I appealed to him as a man alone with a dumb brute so frequently without any thought of aid.

How the hell are we going to get across those cliffs,

Dhani? I asked.

Even though I know that Airedales are incredibly intelligent dogs, I won't say that he understood me. However, I will swear that he appeared to understand me because he wheeled around, barking happily, and trotted off toward the west. When I didn't follow him, he ran back to me, barking furiously, and eventually grabbed my leg by the calf in an attempt to drag me in the direction he wanted me to go. Now that my legs were bare and Dhani' jaws were much stronger than he realised, I gave in and followed him because I realised that, as far as any knowledge I had of the right direction went, I might as well just go.

We travelled a good distance along the cliffs' base. The ground was uneven, covered in trees, and home to a variety of living and extinct herbivores that were grazing singly, in pairs, and in herds. A massive woolly mastodon with enormous upcurving tusks stood moving back and forth in the shade of a huge leaf. A lone rhinoceros dozing in a dust hole was nearby, along with a bull, a cow, and a calf. At the same time, antelope, elephant, horses, sheep, and goats were all visible, and a terrific megatherium leapt up at a distance on its enormous tail and massive hind feet to tear leaves from a tall tree. The forgotten past and the present rubbed shoulders as

Krishna Bisht, the modern of the moderns, passed by dressed as a pre-glacial man, and in front of him trotted a creature of a breed that was probably no older than 60 years. Despite being a parvenu, Dhani showed no signs of concern.

More aerial reptiles and a number of large amphibians were visible as we got closer to the inland sea, but none of them charged at us. In the middle of the afternoon, as we climbed the top, I saw something that caused me to stop abruptly. While I threw myself flat and watched a group of warriors approach the cliff from the south, I called Dhani in a low voice, warned him to be quiet, and kept him at the heel. They were clearly Mahans, and I surmised that Eklavya was in charge. They had overtaken me because they had taken a quicker route to the pass.Since they weren't very far away, I could see them clearly, and I was relieved to see that Maya wasn't with them.

The cliffs in front of them were ragged and broken, with the cliffs emerging from the east extending over the cliffs emanating from the west. The party filed into the encroachment created by this overlapping. For a few minutes, I could see them moving upward before they vanished from view. After the last of them had vanished from view, I got up and started moving toward the pass, which is where Dhani had obviously been directing me.

I went cautiously as I approached the encroachment where I assumed the group was resting. I would have had no concern about being found had they not stopped since I knew the Mahans marched without a point, flanker, or rear guard. However, when I got to the pass and saw a single-man trail snaking upward at an acute angle, I wished I had been the Mahans chief for a few weeks. All the hordes that could be brought up from the south could be held off indefinitely by a dozen men in that narrow pass, yet it was completely unprotected.

Although the Mahans were a great people of Aadra, they were pitifully ineffective in even the most basic military strategies. I was taken aback that even a Stone Age man could be so lacking in military acumen. I observed the shoddy formation of his troop as it crossed an enemy border and entered the realm of the chief against whom he had revolted, Eklavya significantly diminished in my assessment. However, Eklavya must have known Mahamaya the chief and understood that Mahamaya would not be waiting for him at the pass. He nevertheless took unnecessary risks. I could have managed to conquer Aadra with just one team from a home-guard company.

Dhani and I continued on to the top of the pass, where we saw the group entering the Mahan country. The surface of this area was, on average, about a hundred and fifty feet above the nearby Pahadi domain and not much more than fifty feet below the summit of the cliffs. The scenery changed instantly, the shrubs, flowers, and trees were of a hardier variety, I came to the conclusion that a Mahan blanket could be almost indispensable at night. There were a lot of oak and eucalyptus trees, but there were also ash, acorn, pine, redwood, and cedar. Life in the trees was riotous. Massive trees were abundant in the dense forests. From the top of the cliff, I could see forests that rose hundreds of feet above the ground where I was standing, and even from that range, I could tell that the trees there were enormous in size.

I had finally arrived in the Mahan nation. Even though I wasn't born in Aadra, I had grown up from the very beginning, I had passed through the horrifying horrors of the lower Aadraian spheres of evolution. As a result, I could not help but feel some of the joy and pride that Vinasha and Jwala felt when they realised they had been chosen for the call and were about to advance from the inheritance of Gorkhas to that of Pahadis. I was relieved to not be vardhanah.

Where was Maya, though? I searched the vast area in front of me, but all I could see were the Eklavya and his warriors and the animals that lived in the fields and forests. I could see wide plains stretching out across the country, encircled by forests, but there was no indication of a tiny Mahan.

We had not eaten since the previous night, and below us there was competition, sheep, anything a hungry hunter might desire. So, Dhani and I descended the steep trail, and I slithered toward a small flock of red deer feeding at the edge of a plain close to a forest while Dhani crouched low behind me. Lone trees and scattered bushes, provided enough cover for me to easily stalk upwind until I was within 50 feet from my target–a big, svelte doe who was alone with a fawn. I immediately regretted not having my rifle a lot. Although I had never shot an arrow before, I knew how to do it. After attaching the rod to my chain and carefully aiming, I let the arrow go. I called to Dhani and jumped to my legs at the same time.

The outline was hit four-sided by the arrow, and Dhani was immediately after her. She turned to run as the two of us pursued her, Dhani baring his enormous fangs and me holding my short spear ready to cast. The injured doe took longer to move than the rest of the herd, and in a flash, Dhani was standing next to her and lunging for her throat. When I arrived , he had her on the ground, and I used my spear to kill her. It took me very little time to start a fire and cook a steak, and while I was putting the finishing touches on my own feast, Dhani was stuffing himself with raw venison. I've never savoured a meal so much.

I looked in vain for two days, moving northward and back and forth from the inland sea almost to the blocking cliff edges, looking for any sign of Maya. When I saw nothing, not even the group of Mahan warriors led by Eklavya, I started to have doubts. Had Bheeshma told me the truth when he claimed that Maya had left the Pahadi village?

Could he not have been carrying out Shhoor's orders who may have harboured a tiny glimmer of regret over his attempt to kill a he who had made friends with. A Pahadi warrior-a guest who had done no harm to the Pahadi race- and who may have sent me on a fruitless mission in the hopes that the wild animals would act as Shhoor dawdled to? I didn't know, but the more I considered it, the more certain I was that Maya had not left the Pahadi village but if she hadn't why was Eklavya emerged without her? This was a brainteaser, and once more I had no idea what I was doing.

On the second day after my visit to the Mahan region, I came across a herd of horses that were among the most magnificent I had ever seen. They were black bays with white surcingle around their barrels and blazed faces. They had white knees on their forelegs. They were close to sixteen hands tall, with the mares being slightly shorter than the stallions, and numbered three or four among the hundred colts and partially grown horses in this group. Their almost identical markings suggested a pure strain that may have persisted since ancient times. Imagine how I would have felt when I came across these magnificent animals if I had desired one of the little ponies of the Pahadi nation! I made the decision to own one of them as soon as I spotted them, and it didn't take me long to choose a gorgeous young stallion-I estimated him to be four years old.

The horses were eating grass nearby the forest's edge where Dhani and I were hidden, and the ground between us and them was covered in flowering bush and provided excellent cover. The thorough bred of my choice grazed with a mare and two yearlings were closest to the forest and to me, a little apart from the rest of the herd. Dhani squashed himself to the ground in response to my whispered "Charge!" and I knew he wouldn't move again until I called him, unless danger approached me from behind.

I approached my unsuspecting target with caution, sneaking up on him until I was within 20 feet of a bush's cover. I laid out my loop of knots on the ground here, expanding it open and flat. It would only take a moment to step to one side of the bush and throw straight from the floor, which is my preferred method, and in that same moment, the stallion would probably be galloping at full speed in the opposite direction. Then, when I caught him off guard, he would have to wheel around, and as he did so, he would almost certainly lift his head, making a perfect target for my knot as he changed direction.

Yes, I had everything perfectly planned out, and I patiently awaited his turn to approach me. Finally, it became clear that he was acting in this way when the filly suddenly raised her head, neighed, and trotted off in the opposite direction. Of course, the colts and my stallion were right behind her. For a brief moment, it appeared as though my last hope had been dashed, but eventually their fear, if it had been fear, subsided and they started grazing once more a hundred yards away. This time, there was no shrub within fifty feet of them, so I wasn't sure how to get close enough to safely use a rope.

Any place under 40 feet I am a good roper and fair at fifty feet, but I knew it would take luck for me to get my noose around that lovely arched neck above that.

I was almost ready to attempt the long throw as I stood there debating the issue in my head. Given that this Mahan weapon was a full sixty feet in length, I had more than enough rope. How I longed for the ranch's collies! Then it suddenly occurred to me that Dhani had spent the entire summer running with those collies, that he had gone out to the pasture after the cows every evening and contributed to driving them back to the milking barn, and that he had done it intelligently. However, Dhanihad never done the thing alone, and it had been a year since he had done it at all. Even so, the likelihood was higher that I would fumble the long throw than that Dhani would trip and fall if I gave him the opportunity.

After making a choice, I had to sneak back to Dhani and get him before making my way to a big bush close to the four horses with him on my heels. Here, where the bush was directly in our line of sight, I pointed out the animals to Dhani and muttered, "Boy, fetch 'em!"

He quickly disappeared, making a wide circle and heading away from the quarry. They almost immediately noticed him and began to trot away from him, but when they realised that he seemed to be giving them plenty of room, they stopped once more, even as they stood watching him with high-held heads and quivering nostrils. It was a lovely sight. Dhani then turned around and slowly made his way back toward me from behind them. He didn't growl or charge them; instead, he approached them slowly and walked up to them. The magnificent creatures made no attempt to flee until Dhani was quite close to them; after which, they wheeled slowly in the opposite direction.

The wish and worries started right then. Naturally, Dhani tried to turn them, and it appeared that he had chosen the stallion to work on because he paid no attention to the other horses. The stallion was intelligent enough to realise that a solitary dog could run his legs off until he could round up four horses that didn't want to be apprehended. The stallion, on the other hand, had his own ideas about being headed, and the outcome was a race that was as stunning as one could wish to see.

What a fast horse that was! At his forefoot, Dhani ran, doing his best to turn him. He appeared to flatten out and shoot through the air with the barest amount of effort. Now that he was uproaring, he made two high leaps against the stallion's flank. However, this required too much energy and always caused him to lose ground as he was thrown heels over head by the impact. However, before they crossed a rise in the ground, I was certain that Dhani' persistence was paying off because it appeared to me that the horse was yielding a tiny bit to the right. The foal and filly had already retreated to the main herd, and Dhani stood between them.

As I waited for Dhani to return, I couldn't help but consider my chances of being attacked by a powerful animal. I was far from the forest and carrying weapons in which I had little experience, though I had been practicing with the spear ever since I left the Pahadi nation. I must acknowledge that until I had thought of little Maya who was all alone in this same land and only carrying a knife, my thoughts were not satisfying, almost bordering on timidity. I was immediately overcome with shame, but after further reflection, I've come to the conclusion that my mental state was largely influenced by my approximate nakedness.

If you've never walked around in broad daylight while wearing a piece of red deer skin that is too short, you can't possibly understand the sense of futility that overcomes one. When a man is used to wearing clothes, they give him a certain amount of self-assurance; when they are absent, they make him anxious.

However, despite seeing several threatening-looking creatures moving through the forest's shadowy lanes, no beast attacked me. Finally, I started to worry about Dhani' extended absence and worry that something had happened to him. As I was coiling my rope to set out in search of him, I noticed the stallion leap into view almost exactly where he had vanished from view, and Dhani was following closely behind. Neither were moving as quickly or furiously as they had once I last saw them.

As he drew closer to me, I could see that the horse was exerting a lot of effort, but he and Dhani continued to work bravely. The wonderful man was driving the quarry directly in my direction. I knelt down behind my bush and prepared to throw my noose. As the two came closer to where I was hiding, Dhani slowed down, and the stallion, who was obviously only too happy for the break, began to trot. He passed me at this gait, my rope-hand shot forward, the honda held the noose open with its head well down, and the lovely cove fairly ran his nose into it.

He immediately turned to dash off at an angle. With the rope around my hip serving as a brace, I yanked him to a sudden stand. He struggled and resisted for his freedom as Dhani came and knelt down next to me while panting his tongue hanging out.

He appeared to understand that his work was finished and that he deserved to relax. The stallion was pretty worn out by this point, and after a few minutes of battling, he stood with his feet apart, his eyes wide, and his nostrils dilated, watching me as I crept closer to him, taking in the slack in the rope as I went. He raised and attempted to escape a dozen times, but each time I comforted him, and after an hour of work, I was able to reach his head and stroke his muzzle. I gave him a handful of grass after that and continued to speak to him in a soothing tone of voice.

In contrast to what I had anticipated, I discovered that taming him was relatively simple. Although wild, he was somewhat gentle and extremely intelligent, and he quickly realised that I had no desire to hurt him. Everything was simple after that. Before the day was over, I had successfully trained him to take charge, stand still while I stroked his head and flanks, and eat from my hand. I also had the pleasure of watching the fear fade from his big, perceptive eyes.

The next day I decided to make a hackamore out of a piece I cut off the end of my long Mahan rope and mounted him, ready for a battle of massive proportions in which I was not entirely confident that he would prevail. However, he made not the slightest attempt to unseat me, and from that point on his training was quick. No horse has ever picked up on the significance of the rein and the stress from the knees more rapidly. While he and Dhani were the best of friends, I believe he soon came to love me and I know that I did. I referred to him as Varuna. When Varuna let himself out, he undoubtedly flew, according to a friend of mine who once served in the Indian flying corps.

Without being a horseman yourself, you won't be able to fully comprehend or understand what an exhilarating sense of well-being I experienced as soon as I started riding Agni. I was a brand-new man, filled with a superiority complex that made me believe I could take on all of Aadra by myself. Now, whenever I was in need of meat, I would run Agni down and rope him. When a large beast that we could not handle threatened us, we galloped away to safety. However, for the most part, the creatures we encountered regarded Agni and I with awe because we represented a novel and strange beast that was beyond their comprehension.

I drove straight and forth through the southern part of the Mahan country for five days without encountering a single person. Despite this, I was slowly making my way north because I was determined to thoroughly search the area for Maya. However, on the fifth day, as I emerged from a forest, I spotted a single small figure being pursued by many others. I knew the quarry was right away to Maya. The entire group was crossing my path at right angles and was more than a mile away from me, with

Maya leading the way by a few hundred yards. One of her chasers had gotten a head start on the others and was closing the distance quickly. I gave Agni the command to jump straight into the open with a word and an ankle stress. With Dhani running closely behind, we sped toward her.

Initially, none of them noticed us, but as we got closer to Maya, the pack leader saw us and let out a howl I had never heard before. All of them were Mahans, and I soon identified the leader as Eklavya.

He was now almost upon Maya, and I saw him running with his knife in his hand, intending to kill rather than capture. I sensed terror I had never before felt. I was unable to comprehend it, and all I could do was urge Agni to move more quickly. The amazing animal complied with my requests most honourably. Agni was the closest a four-legged animal had ever come to flying on that day.

Eklavya was not noticing towards us because he was focused on his brutal design. He was just a pace away from Maya when Agni and I dashed between them. I swept my little barbarian into the hollow of my arm and up on the withers of the glorious Agni while stooping to the left. We had rescued her from Eklavya's grasp, who had halted, confused, and furious. Maya was perplexed as well because we had approached her from the side and she had no idea we were close until she was started swinging to Agni's back.

When her eyes caught my face and she recognised me, the little brute turned with her knife drawn and prepared to stab me. She gasped as she wrapped her arms around my neck and sobbed a little "My Krishna! My Krishna!"

Maya and I were lobbed far over Agni's head when he suddenly submerged himself to his belly in a patch of thick mud. He had collided with one of the many springs that cover Aadra. They can be tiny lakes, small pools, or even just mud bogs, like this one, which was covered in lush grasses and thus effectively concealed its perilous nature. Given how quickly Agni was moving when he fell, it's amazing he didn't break a leg, even though he was unable to crawl out of the muck with his four healthy legs. Although Maya and I had lain face down in the surrounding grasses, we had not sunk far. However, when we tried to stand up, we discovered that there was no solid ground, and soon we noticed that Eklavya and his followers were approaching us. No way out existed. It was clear that we would perish.

"Kill me," Maya begged. "Instead of having this hateful thing's knife kill me, let me die in your loved hands. He has vowed to murder me. He held me captive last night, and when he tried to have his way with me, I attacked him with my fists and assaulted him with my knife, and then I ran away, leaving him writhing in pain and frustrated desire. They found me today after searching for me, and as I was fleeing, Eklavya pursued me while wailing that he would kill me. Kill me, my Krishna, and then fall upon your own spear; if they take you alive, they will kill you dreadfully." I tried to tell her that I loved her and that I would fight for her until death came but I couldn't tell her this, not until it was too late.

Dhani had ventured into the bog after us and had performed admirably at first, but as he got closer to us, he too sank to his belly and could do nothing but flounder. When Eklavya and his disciples approached the edge of the terrifying swamp, we were in this situation. I noticed that Shhoor and numerous other Pahadi warriors were also with him. The alliance against Mahamaya the chief had been finalised, and the horde was already approaching the Mahan city. I sighed as I realised how close I had come to preventing not only the death and defeat of Maya's father and his people, but also of Maya herself.

A thick wood was located beyond the swamp. We would have been secure had we made it there, but it might as well have been a hundred miles away as a hundred yards across that muddy lake that was hidden from view. Eklavya and his horde stopped at the edge of the swamp to mock us. They were unable to reach us with their hands, but when Eklavya ordered them to do so, they equipped their bows with arrows, and I knew that the battle was over. Maya huddled up next to me, so I grabbed her and held her. She declared, "Krishna, you are the only one I love." Then, instead of tears of self-pity for my situation, tears of great love-from a heart that observes the sun of its life and its love trying to set even as it rises-came to my eyes.

When the pleasant music that has ever been heard by man suddenly erupted from the wood beyond the swamp, the renegade Mahans and their Pahadi allies were waiting for the word from Eklavya that would launch that barbed avalanche of death upon us. It was the sharp percussive of at least two score carbines fired rapidly and at will. Before that lethal fusillade, the warriors of the Mahan and Pahadi fell like tenpins.

What might it indicate? I took it to mean only one thing: that mahan, pahadi and the others had managed to scale cliffs and travel to the Mahan region on the other side of the island in time to save Maya and me from an almost certain demise. I didn't need to know them well to recognise the men holding those rifles as members of my own party, and when they emerged from hiding a short while later, my eyes confirmed my suspicions. Every man-jack of them was there, along with a thousand sleek, straight soldiers of the Mahan race. Before others, two men showed up dressed in Mahans gown.

Each one of them was tall, straight, and gorgeously muscled, but they were unique in the same way Agni might be. Maya stretched out her arms and cried as they got closer to the muck "Mahamaya, my lord! father!" and the older of the two dove in knee-deep swamp water to save her. Then, as the other drew near and peered into my face, both his and my eyes widened, and I cried out: "Vishvesh! Vishvesh Sudarshana, for the love of God!"

He was there. My quest was over. All of my friends and the man we had searched the entire new world for were gathered around me. Before they could free the three of us, they cut down trees in the forest and paved a path through the swamp. We then marched back to Mahamaya, the Mahan chief's city, where there was a great celebration when Maya rode home once more on the lustrous back of the thoroughbred Agni.

On the way back to the town, Sudarshana, Farhan, Naagar, and the rest of the Indians nearly made our jaws fall out. We continued doing so for days afterward. They explained to me how they had traversed the barrier cliffs in five days by working three eight-hour shifts for a total of twenty-four hours each day, with two reliefs to each shift switching off every half-hour. Drilling two holes four feet apart in the cliff face and in the same horizontal planes were two men using electric drills powered by the dynamos on the Jalayana.

The holes had a slight downward slope. After laying a plank across these two holes and inserting iron rods that were specifically brought for this purpose as part of our equipment, the next shift mounted to the new level and bored two additional gaps five feet just above new platform, and so forth.

The Jalayana's searchlights were kept on facing the cliff where the drills were located throughout the nights, and on the fifth day, was managed to reach the summit at a rate of ten feet per hour. Except for the few men needed to man the Jalayana, ropes were lowered, blocks were fastened to trees at the top, and rudimentary elevators were rigged, so by the evening of the fifth day, the entire party-including a large quantity of weapons, ammo, and equipment were inside Aadra.

They then made a desperate and dangerous attempt to cross into the horrifying, reptile-infested territory to the south before fighting their way north in search of me. Their path was littered with the dead creatures they had been determined to shoot to win their way to the north end of the island, where they had found Vishvesh and his wife among the Mahans of Mahamaya. However, because they had so many guns, they had not lost a single man.

Vishvesh and Dhani' reunion was marked by a frenzied display from Dhani that almost cost Vishvesh the scanty clothing that the Mahan custom had granted him. Pinal was waiting to greet us when we got to the Mahan city.

Although neither Pinal nor Vishvesh would admit that a civil or religious ceremony could have made the bonds with which God had allied them more sacred, she was now Mrs. Sudarshana because the master of the Jalayana had married them on the same day that that the search party had discovered them.

Agnivesh and his group had not made themselves known to Vishvesh or the Jalayana party. Since they had been missing for such a long time, all hope for them had to be given up. The Western Pahadi, the Gorkha, and the Mahans had all heard of them, but no one had actually seen them even though they had left Fort Dinosaur months earlier.

For a fortnight, we rested in Mahamaya's village before getting ready to travel south to the location where the Jalayana would be waiting for us. Bheeshma, a now-full-fledged Mahan, arrived from the Pahadi country during these two weeks. He informed us that when Shhoor's party attempted to enter Pahadi again, they were killed. After becoming chief, Bheeshma left the tribe with a new leader that everyone respected.

While Agni, Maya, and I took numerous long journeys through the stunning north Mahan country, Dhani stayed close to Vishvesh. My clothes were gone, but Bheeshma had brought my arms and ammo up from Pahadi with him, so I didn't miss them once I got used to the Mahan way of dressing.

Finally, the time had come for us to leave; the next morning, we were to depart for the south, the Jalayana, and beloved Dweep behind Maya's father Mahamaya had rejected my request for her to accompany us, even though I had made the request. No appeals could convince him to change his mind; Maya, the Vishesh, who might give rise to a more superior and newer Aadraian race, could not be exempted. I could have any other Mahans woman, but not Maya.

The poor kid was devastated, and as for me, I was beginning to understand how much of a hold Maya had on my heart and started to wonder how I would manage without her. When I finally tore myself away and went to my own hut to snatch a few hours of sleep before we set out on our long journey the following day, I consoled myself with the thought that time would heal the wound and that back in my native land I would find a mate who would be all and more. I had finally realised that I loved her - loved my little barbarian; and as I tried to imagine what life would be like without her. Morning arrived faster than I could have anticipated. I got up and had breakfast, but Maya was not there. I reasoned that it would be best for me to leave without experiencing the agonising pain of saying goodbye. The group organised for the march and prepared an escort of Mahan warriors to go with us. Even going to Agni's place to say goodbye to him was beyond my ability to bear. I had given him to Maya the previous evening, and in my mind, the two were now essential.

Therefore, we marched off down the block flanked by cottages, through the wide gateway in the city's stone wall, and across the clearing toward the forest that we had to pass through to get to Mahan's northern boundary, after which we would turn south. When I turned to look back at the city that held my heart at the edge of the forest, I caught sight of what abruptly stopped me in my tracks. It was the large gateway.

It was a small, crinkled figure leaning against one of the large upright posts that the gates swing upon. Even from this distance, I could see its shoulders heave with the rage of its sobs. It was the clincher.

I was close to Vishvesh. I bid the old man farewell. I'm returning, I say.

He gave me a startled look. He took my hand and said, "Good-bye, old man." "I predicted you'd pull it off in the end."

When the last of the anti-Indians had vanished into the forest, Maya and I watched it together as I went back and took her in my arms, kissing the tears from her eyes and a smile to her lips.

*****